D1626033

AT THE CHATEAU
FOR CHRISTMAS

AT THE CHATEAU
FOR CHRISTMAS

BY

REBECCA WINTERS

First published in Great Britain 2014
by Mills & Boon, an imprint of Harlequin (UK) Limited,
Large Print edition 2015
Eton House, 18-24 Paradise Road,
Richmond, Surrey, TW9 1SR

© 2014 Rebecca Winters

ISBN: 978-0-263-25612-3

Harlequin (UK) Limited's policy is to use papers that are natural, renewable and recyclable products and made from wood grown in sustainable forests. The logging and manufacturing processes conform to the legal environmental regulations of the country of origin.

Printed and bound in Great Britain
by CPI Antony Rowe, Chippenham, Wiltshire

Dedicated to
my two wonderful grandmothers,
Alice Driggs Brown and Rebecca Ormsby Hyde.

I had these grandmothers in my life
until just a few years ago and consider them
two of life's greatest blessings.

CHAPTER ONE

THE FINANCIAL DISTRICT of San Francisco was known as the Wall Street of the West. Nic got out of the limo into sunny, fifty-eight-degree weather and entered the high-rise that housed the headquarters of Holden Hotels on Montgomery.

There might be no snow in this city by the bay, but Americans were big on Christmas trees. The tall one in the foyer decorated with pink bows, pink angels and pink lights was dazzling. The hotel chain started by Richard Holden had become one of California's finest.

Nic had checked in to one near the airport upon his arrival at 3:00 p.m., a half hour ago. A smaller tree decorated the same way with a giant Santa Claus in the corner had illuminated its foyer. He was impressed by its unmatched American ambience that would enchant children of all ages and nationalities. Once it might have enchanted him, but no longer. These days Christmas was a painful holiday he had to get through.

A security guard at reception in the lounge of the foyer looked up at him. "May I help you, sir?"

"I hope so. I'm here to see Ms. Laura Holden Tate. I understand she's manager of the marketing department."

"Do you have an appointment?"

"No. I'm here on urgent business and must speak to her as soon as possible."

"Your name?"

"Monsieur Valfort. She'll recognize the name."

"One moment, please, and I'll ring her secretary."

Nic had to wait a few minutes for an answer. The man gave him a speculative glance before he said, "If you'll take a seat, she'll be down shortly."

So she was in…that was good. Saved him from having to hunt her down.

The name *Valfort* had probably given Ms. Tate a heart attack. He'd purposely left off his first name to keep her guessing. But Nic wasn't surprised she was willing to drop everything in order to investigate this undesirable intrusion away from the eyes and ears of her staff. He had to admit he'd been curious about a woman who'd shown no interest or love, let alone curiosity, over her grandmother's welfare all these years. It demonstrated a coldness he couldn't comprehend.

"Please help yourself to coffee while you wait."

"Thank you." Except that Nic didn't want coffee and didn't feel like sitting. He'd done enough of both on the flight from Nice, France, which, being on the Côte d'Azur, showed no signs of snow and coincidentally had been fifty-eight degrees and sunny when he'd left.

The errand his grandfather Maurice had sent him on was one he wanted over. He wasn't looking forward to this meeting, let alone the other business his grandfather had asked him to carry out.

There would be fireworks, but with so many people coming in and out of the building, he planned to convince Ms. Tate to talk to him away from everyone. If this woman was as bitter and unforgiving as her mother, then he had his work cut out.

He looked in the direction of the bank of elevators, braced for a confrontation. Every time he heard the ding, he watched another group of well-dressed people step out. Though he didn't have a picture of Ms. Tate, he knew she was a midlevel executive, twenty-seven years old and had been born with blond hair. Not a great deal to go on. At this point all he could do was wait until she approached him.

When he decided something must have detained her, he suddenly noticed an ash-blond woman with silky hair to the shoulders of her chic navy suit walking in his direction from the stairway door on long, shapely legs.

Out of nowhere Nic felt an unbidden rush of physical attraction. Not in years had that kind of powerful reaction to a woman happened to him.

This was the woman he'd flown all these miles to talk to?

Maybe he was wrong and she was meeting someone else, but no one else was standing by him. On closer inspection he noticed that her coloring and five-foot-seven-inch height could have been the way her grandmother Irene Holden would have looked at the same age. Irene had been an exceptionally beautiful woman.

Nic stood there stunned by the strong family resemblance. That had to explain why he'd been so taken with the woman's looks. She had a certain elegance, like her grandmother, and wore white pearls around her neck as he'd seen Irene do many times. Their sheen was reflected in her hair.

The similarity of the two women's classic features was uncanny, though the granddaughter's mouth was a little fuller. *Her mouth...and her eyes...* They were a lighter blue than her grandmother's.

But instead of the hint of wistfulness that was Irene's trademark, he saw guarded hostility as her granddaughter's gaze swept over him with patent disdain.

"I'm Laura Tate. Which of the Valfort men are you?"

Nothing like coming straight to the point with such an acerbic question, but he was prepared.

"Nicholas. My grandfather Maurice married your grandmother Irene."

He heard her take a quick extra breath. Much to his chagrin, it drew his attention to the voluptuous figure no expensive, classy business suit could hide. She was Irene's granddaughter, all right.

"Paul told me your business was urgent. It must be a life-and-death situation for you to make the long flight into the enemy camp."

Nic changed his mind. This woman wasn't anything like her delightful grandmother, which made him more irritated with himself than ever over his unexpected physical reaction to her.

"I'd rather talk to you outside in the limo, where we won't have an audience." He sensed her hesitation. "I'm not here to abduct you," he asserted. "That isn't the Valfort way, *despite* the rumors in your family."

He noticed how her jaw hardened, but ignored the grimace and got down to the business of why he'd come. "I'm here to inform you that your grandmother passed away day before yesterday, at St. Luc's Hospital in Nice."

The second the news left his lips, Laura's facade crumbled for a moment. In that instant her whole demeanor changed, like a flower that had lost its moisture. He knew he'd delivered a message that had rocked her world. For no reason he could understand, he felt a trace of compassion for her. Tears sprang to those crystalline eyes, bringing out his protective instincts despite his initial resentment of her lack of feeling for her own grandmother.

"My grandfather wanted you and your mother to hear the news in person. Since he knew he wouldn't be welcome here, he asked me to come in his place. If you'll walk out to the limo—the most convenient meeting place I could devise—I'll tell you everything."

Irene Holden had been his grandfather's

raison d'être. Nic was still trying to deal with the recent loss himself. He'd loved Irene, who'd been a big part of his life. Her death had left a huge void, one this unfeeling granddaughter couldn't possibly comprehend.

Was it true? The grandmother she'd hardly known was *dead*?

If Laura were the type, she would have fainted. This tall, striking Frenchman dressed in an expensive charcoal-colored silk suit and tie had just delivered unexpected news that shook her to the very foundation.

He had to be in his early thirties and wore a wedding ring. She'd noticed something else— Nicholas Valfort spoke excellent English with a seductive French accent, no doubt just like the rogue grandfather who'd beguiled her grandmother. A man like this had no right to be so... appealing.

Is that what had happened to Irene—she'd felt an overwhelming attraction to Maurice the moment she'd met him? Like granddaughter, like grandmother?

The surreal moment made it difficult for Laura to function, let alone breathe, but she had to.

Without further urging on Nicholas's part, she followed him to the front of the building. Once he'd helped her into the back of the limousine, he sat across from her.

She had an impression of vibrant black hair and hard-boned features, but all she could focus on were the moody gray eyes beneath black brows, studying her as if she were an unpleasant riddle he couldn't solve and frankly didn't want to.

"I brought these pictures of her with me. Please feel free to keep them. They were taken in the last year before she became so ill with pneumonia."

Laura groaned. *Pneumonia?*

He opened an envelope on the seat and handed her half a dozen five-by-seven color photos. Five of them showed her grandmother alone in different outdoor settings. The last one had caught her standing in a garden with a man who had to be her second husband, Maurice.

The same Valfort characteristics of height and

musculature in the photo had been bequeathed to the arresting male seated across from Laura. But unlike him, the man's hair in the picture had turned silver.

She studied the photos for a long time. Her grandmother had still been beautiful at eighty. Pain caused her throat to constrict.

"I brought her body on the Valfort corporate jet. Maurice called the Sunset Mortuary here in San Francisco to meet the plane. Here's their business card." She took it from him, cognizant of their fingers touching. Something was wrong with her to be this aware of him when she was in so much turmoil.

"They're awaiting your family's instructions. When your mother broke all ties with Irene, she told her that neither she nor my grandfather would ever be welcome at her home in this life."

Searing pain shot through Laura. Her mother had said those exact words to Laura's grandmother? Laura didn't believe it. This man was biased and had colored the situation with his own judgmental version of the scandal. Still, it was so horrifying, the tragedy of it all over-whelmed her.

"My grandfather is still honoring her wishes, thus the reason I'm here in his place."

That was another lie. His grandfather was a coward or he would have come himself!

"Maurice realizes your grandmother should be buried next to her first husband, Richard, and surrounded by her family."

So in death Richard was finally remembered? The heat of anger and pain washed over her. "How thoughtful of him." She hadn't been able to hide the sarcasm.

Calmly he said, "If you have questions and need to talk to me, I'll be staying at the airport Holden Hotel. You can reach me there until to-morrow morning, when I'll be flying back to Nice at seven a.m.

"One more thing. Your grandmother had a will drawn up several years ago and left some-thing specific in it for you. Unfortunately it means you will have to fly to Nice and meet with the attorney within the next seven days. After that, he'll be out of the country for two months. It was her hope that your mother's feelings wouldn't prevent you from claiming it. She never gave up hope of a reconciliation."

At the revelation, Laura couldn't stifle a quiet sob.

"Should you decide to come, phone me and I'll arrange for the Valfort jet to return to San Francisco and fly you to Nice. My grandfather insists on doing this for you to honor Irene's final wishes. I'll meet you at the Nice airport and drive you directly to the attorney's office. This is my business card." He handed it to her. "You can reach me at Valfort Technologies any time."

He didn't work for the fabulously wealthy Valfort family? They'd been hoteliers since the early 1900s. That much she did know about them. Why on earth would he stay in a Holden hotel after what his grandfather had done to their family? Or did he have a sick desire to see how the Holdens were doing business without the founder?

"Do you have any questions, Ms. Tate?"

At this point her emotions were in chaos.

"Only two right now." She fought to keep the tremor out of her voice, but to her alarm, she had difficulty keeping her eyes off him. "Did you know her well?"

"Very" came the grating sound of his voice.

Laura sensed a wealth of meaning and possible rebuke behind that one word, stabbing her until she could feel herself bleeding out. But this man knew nothing about the private history of the Holden family and the horrendous gulf caused by his grandfather. She bristled at his unspoken censure of her.

Narrowing her eyes on him she said, "Am I to assume she was happy with your grandfather?"

"With *him,* absolutely."

What exactly was *that* supposed to mean? "That's your interpretation, of course."

She got no response from him. His sangfroid crept under her skin. So did his lack of explanation that spoke volumes about the underlying issues of a marriage that had brought so much grief to her mother and to Laura personally.

Laura averted her eyes, needing to exit the limo and be strictly alone while she absorbed the gut-wrenching news about her grandmother's death.

All these years without contact. Laura hadn't seen Irene since she was six. Year after year she'd secretly yearned to visit her and get to know her. But loyalty to her mother, Jessica, had prevented her from getting in touch with her. Now the lovely older woman in the photos was gone... *Death was irrevocable.*

Another small sob escaped her throat. She traced her grandmother's features with her index finger. These few pictures were all Laura would ever have of the woman who'd brought her mother into the world and raised her. The pain of loss over an opportunity never seized was excruciating. How empty and pointless that loyalty seemed now.

Without lashing out at her, Laura would have to search her soul to find the right words to tell her unforgiving mother that Irene was dead. She lifted her head, looking at Nicholas through dull eyes. Tears trickled down her throat, yet it was hard to swallow.

"It's evident this was a task you would have

done anything to avoid. Your loyalty to your grandfather deserves a medal. I suppose the least I can do is thank you for tearing yourself away from business to come all this way with her body."

"You're welcome."

His cool reply had her floundering. Clearly this man found his errand repugnant. But as much as she knew anything, she realized he was a true gentleman, a quality she valued highly in a man. Otherwise he would have flung all this in her face with the greatest of pleasure. His restraint taught her a lot about his character, adding to the potent charisma no man of her acquaintance possessed.

He got out of the back to help her. As her body brushed against his by accident, an unlooked-for awareness of his male presence leaped to life, threatening her in ways she'd never experienced before. The knowledge that he was married only made her reaction to him that much more shocking. She clutched the photos and cards before running toward the building without looking back.

* * *

"Telephone, Nic. Line two."

Nic had been making corrections to a drawing on the computer. "*Merci,* Robert."

After three years, his stomach no longer clenched every time a call came through for him, whether it was on his cell or the landline at work. For the first year following his wife's disappearance, he'd imagined every call would be from Lt. Thibault, the investigating detective on the other end, phoning to give him news of Dorine.

"It's five. I'm heading home and will see you after Christmas."

That's right. It was December 23. Nic's assistant, Robert, was going home to a wife and two children. Nic wouldn't be going home to anyone. Except to spend a little time with his family and siblings, he would work through this holiday.

Three years ago he and Dorine had spent Christmas with her family in Grenoble. They'd only been married five months before her disappearance in January. Their marriage had been of too short a duration to put down roots with children.

Robert paused at the door. "Thanks for the gifts. Pierre and Nicole will love them."

He lifted his head. "My pleasure."

"Nic—everyone at the research park is hoping *Père Noël* will bring some news that will give you closure, *mon ami*."

"After three years that hope is all but gone, but I appreciate the thought. *Joyeux Noël*."

Once the door closed, he pressed line two, putting the call on speakerphone while he worked. "This is Nic Valfort."

"Mr. Valfort? This is Laura Tate."

His head flew back, recognizing her California accent. That was another trait she had in common with Irene. Instead of forgetting this woman, to his amazement she'd managed to intrude into his thoughts. Up until he'd flown to San Francisco, his love for Dorine and the reason for her disappearance had been the only things on his mind.

Several times in the limo parked in front of Holden headquarters over a week ago, he'd heard little sobs catch in her throat. He'd had difficulty reconciling Ms. Tate's icy demeanor at one moment and the tears that welled in her eyes in the next. She was an enigma he didn't want to think about. There'd been no word from her since they'd talked.

To his chagrin the two questions she'd asked him had left an indelible impression. Once he'd told her he knew Irene well, her question about her grandmother's happiness with Maurice had haunted him. Had it been a ploy to convince him she cared when she didn't? Had she hoped to give the impression she wasn't the unfeeling person he'd imagined when they both knew the truth?

The seven-day window he'd given her to meet with the attorney had already closed, so he couldn't understand why she was calling.

"Is this a bad time, Mr. Valfort?"

Bad wasn't the right word. More that he'd been in a state of grief-stricken limbo for an endless period of time without knowing the whereabouts of his wife. If she'd run off with another man, he was still having trouble believing it. The woman he'd fallen in love with couldn't have done it, but his sessions with the psychiatrist convinced him it was possible.

Any other reasons why she'd disappeared had tortured him for so long he was desperate for any news, no matter how ghastly, in order to have closure. As for his grandfather, he was in bad emotional shape for another reason. Maurice had lost two women he'd loved and married. In his grief for Irene, he didn't know what to do with himself.

Both womanless men made a pitiful pair. Might as well answer this woman's question with one of his own. "What can I do for you, Ms. Tate?"

"Am I too late to meet with the attorney?"

He grimaced. She couldn't manage to see her grandmother in life, but she wanted to know what her grandmother had left her in death. How predictable. "You've missed the deadline by two days. He's already left on vacation."

A small cry of frustration escaped her throat. "I was afraid of that. Because of some personal matters and the graveside service for her, I couldn't get here any sooner."

His thoughts reeled. "Here? As in—"

"I'm at the airport in Nice."

Nic's adrenaline kicked in for no good reason. He jumped up from his swivel chair in surprise. "How did you get here? On a commercial plane?" She hadn't called to arrange for the Valfort jet.

"The way most people do."

Most people? "Not the Holden corporate jet?"

"I'm not that high up the chain."

"Not yet, you mean."

"In other words you're assuming I'm an ambitious female working my way up to the top of the Holden Corporation. Haven't you learned yet? It's still a man's world in certain venues. Shall we get straight to the point? Your grandfather was decent enough to take care of the arrangements for my grandmother and send you to do his errand. That was more than my family could ever have expected. But I would never have taken him up on his offer to fly me here."

Nic's brows furrowed in resentment. Maurice

had bent over backward trying to do the right thing. "It's too bad you've wasted a trip. Call me in two months. By then the attorney will be back and you can make arrangements to collect your inheritance."

"Whatever you insist on believing, I have no interest in one." After a slight pause, she said, "I should have phoned first, but as you say, it's too late now. Before I turn around and fly back, do you think your grandfather would accept a phone call from me? Or is his opinion of me as bad as yours?"

That all depended on how grasping she was. If she thought she could get Maurice to tell her what her grandmother had left her in the will before the attorney could read it to her, then she was in for a big surprise.

"Hello? Mr. Valfort? Are you still there?"

"Yes." But he wasn't sure he wanted her to talk to his grandfather right off. Maurice had tender feelings for Irene's granddaughter even though he'd never met her. Nic didn't want him hurt because Laura hadn't inherited Irene's sweetness. Death had a way of making all of them vulnerable one way or another. He needed to vet her first.

"My grandfather isn't available right now. Give me fifteen minutes and I'll pick you up at the airport terminal."

"That won't be necessary. I'll go to a hotel to call him and fly home in the morning."

"I'm afraid it's very necessary if you hope to make contact with him."

"You mean I have to get past you first."

He bit down hard. "He's in deep grief, Ms. Tate. I want to protect him. You and I need to talk first, but not over the phone."

That seemed to take her by surprise. "Well, if you're sure you don't mind—"

Mind? She could have no idea how determined he was to find out what she was up to.

"My grandfather would expect me to accommodate you."

"But this will be putting you out."

Now she was going polite on him? He frowned. Was it part of her act? Whatever, she was doing a good job of it. "Au contraire. Since you want to talk to him, something I didn't expect from you, my grandfather would never forgive me if I ignored your request and let you get away."

Nic hated to admit it to himself, but he was curious to see her again. Maybe the second time around she wouldn't impact him in the same way as before. It was something he had to find out.

A pause ensued. "I know this is another one of those tasks you don't want to do."

He let go of the breath he was holding. "You're wrong. This is the one Christmas present my grandfather hadn't counted on." If she was sincere, her arrival might just have saved Maurice from falling into a slump he'd never climb out of. Nic needed time to find out if avarice had brought her here or not. "Watch for me in front of the terminal. I'll be driving a four-door black Mercedes."

"I'll be there."

He heard the click. Making one of his gut decisions, Nic decided to take her to his house. That way no one in his family would know what was going on. Their disapproval of Maurice marrying a foreigner had never truly gone away.

Now the gorgeous granddaughter had arrived. Out of the frying pan…

Laura's physical resemblance to Irene would be a doubly powerful reminder of the woman who'd captured Maurice's heart. Depending on the outcome, more underlying animosity was in store. This had to be handled discreetly for now. Nic and his grandfather had always enjoyed a certain affinity. His loyalty to the older man had never been in question and he wasn't about to desert him now.

Since his grandfather wouldn't be eating dinner for several hours yet, Nic would make the phone call from his den once she was ensconced. They'd proceed from there.

He drove out of his parking spot and wound around the technology park to the main road leading to the airport. Day before yesterday he'd decided he wouldn't be hearing from Ms. Tate again, but he hadn't had the heart to tell his grandfather yet. Now he wouldn't have to.

Though the sun had set, she wasn't difficult to spot. Like Irene, she had incredible dress sense. When Nic pulled up to the terminal, he saw that

Laura drew a lot of attention in a long-sleeved speckled-tweed jacket and slim skirt. The form-fitting dove-gray outfit had white lace appliqués and fringe trim on the jacket. The effect, combined with the silvery-gold glints in her hair, had captured *his* attention.

Her impact on him was even more forceful than the first time. He levered himself from the car and walked around. She carried only one suitcase. Nic helped her inside and stowed it in the backseat. A light, flowery fragrance assailed his senses. "You travel light."

"I didn't plan to be here more than a few days. Thank you for coming to get me, Mr. Valfort." That sounded halfway sincere.

"Nic." He was tired of the senseless formality.

"In that case, call me Laura. I made reservations ahead of time at the Boscolo Excedra. If you wouldn't mind dropping me there." That five-star hotel had recently been restored with a futuristic-themed bar. No surprise she knew about it.

"My grandfather wouldn't hear of it. Maurice

asked me to take care of you before I left for California. For the time being, you'll stay at my home. I'll drive you there now and we'll get in touch with him."

Nic felt her glance. "Does your wife know you'll be bringing someone home with you? No woman likes to be unprepared for an unexpected guest."

She'd noticed his wedding ring, of course. He pulled into traffic. "As it happens, my wife is away for the present." She *was* away, maybe somewhere still on earth, but more likely in heaven. He had no proof of either status. "My staff will see to your comfort. If Dorine were here, she'd want to meet you."

His wife hadn't been a Valfort and she'd liked Irene very much. At this point he realized he'd been thinking of Dorine in the past tense for a long time now. No stone had been unturned, no expense had been too great to find out what had happened to her, but there'd been no trace. During the first year, he'd lived for news of her. But for the last two years, he'd had the feeling in his gut she was gone forever. *Like Irene...*

Before long he took a turnoff and entered a wooded area that led to his home overlooking the coast. Dorine had loved the setting on sight and begged him to buy it before their wedding took place. Not too small, not too large. Perfect for several children who hadn't had time to come along. Empty as a tomb with no one home except the efficient husband-and-wife staff who took care of things.

Provence come to life!

This villa with its red-tiled roof looked like one of the fabulous Provençal properties featured in high-end magazines sold throughout the world. Laura's eyelids smarted with salty tears when she realized Irene would have been here many times enjoying the cypress trees and view of the blue Mediterranean.

Laura had traveled to Europe on several occasions and had been to Paris, but she'd avoided the South of France for fear the temptation to drop in on her grandmother would be too great.

What a colossal fool she'd been to honor her mother's wishes to such a great extent! In doing so she'd denied herself the opportunity to know the woman Laura's grandfather Richard had loved and married.

"Does your mother know you've come?" Nic's deep voice broke in on her anguished thoughts.

"Yes." She bit her lip. "She couldn't stop me. We had a fight."

"You mean she tried to?"

"Yes, but I refused to listen. I told Mother she was inhuman to be upset with me now that Irene was dead. I wish I hadn't said it, but I did. Now I have another regret to live with."

There'd been unpleasantness with Adam, too. The man she'd been seeing over the last few months hadn't wanted her to leave without him. He was getting much too serious. This unexpected trip would give her a needed break from him over the holidays.

His aggression had made her uncomfortable. Maybe her mom had been right—she'd hinted that Adam was ambitious and wanted more than her love. After the way he'd reacted before she'd flown here, Laura had begun to fear the same thing, considering a fortune lay behind her name. Because of the painful history that had beset the Holden family, she had major trust issues. Laura wasn't sure she wanted to be with him anymore.

"Family loyalty has its price," Nic murmured, sounding distanced. "You'd be surprised how many times in the past I had to stop myself from phoning to demand you come and visit your grandmother. She loved you a great deal, but my grandfather wouldn't have approved, so I didn't act on my instincts. He always hoped you'd come on your own."

His admission tugged at her heart. "No matter how much I love my mother, I should have followed my instincts, too. Now it's too late." She moaned the words. "Sometimes family loyalty demands too much, in this case more than I can bear—"

At this point she had the impression he didn't know if he could believe anything she said. That was trouble with a tragedy that had torn families apart. She didn't know if she could believe anything he said, either, but she was here now.

For the sake of the grandmother she'd always loved in her heart, she wanted some answers.

Laura got out of his car before he could help her. The best thing she could do was avoid getting too close so they couldn't possibly touch. Despite his poor opinion of her, she was afraid her attraction to him wasn't going to go away. It was madness that she felt this awareness of him. He was a married man, for heaven's sake!

Nic reached for her suitcase and walked her to the entrance. The minute he opened the door to the foyer, a large manger scene placed on the credenza greeted her vision. Moving on into the living room, it felt as though she'd stepped into a painting by Matisse, her favorite Impressionist.

The interior reminded her of his work *The Black Table.* Wonderful dark flooring and beams set a backdrop for flowers, blue-and-white-colored prints, priceless ceramics and paintings. Beyond the French doors was a view of the sea dotted with sailboats, even though it was winter.

She wheeled around. "Your home is wonderful!" The compliment flew out of her mouth without conscious thought.

"Thank you." He lowered her suitcase. The man had a brooding sophistication he didn't seem to be aware of. "If you'd like to freshen up, there's a bathroom off the guest bedroom on your left at the end of the hall."

"Thank you."

"Are you hungry? Thirsty?"

"I ate before I got off the plane, but maybe some coffee?"

"I'll ask my housekeeper to prepare it and take your bag to your room."

He was giving her the opportunity to compose herself. Nic had his emotions well under control—unlike Laura—and seemed to sense instinctively what she needed. The consummate host.

On her way back to the living room, she stopped to look at the photographs hanging in the hallway. One of the groupings caught her interest. The French-looking brunette in the photos had to be his wife. She was a cute little thing with stylish short hair. They were laughing together.

Laura couldn't imagine feeling that happy and carefree. It depressed her that she'd never had a relationship like that. The more she thought about it, the more she knew she would have to end it with Adam. They didn't bring out the best in each other. Look at the way Nic and his wife glowed in the photograph. You could feel their happiness.

Upset by her thoughts, she returned to the front room and found a tray of coffee and variety of cookies waiting for her. Nic was on the phone speaking his native tongue and stood behind one of the two sofas facing each other. Separating them was a tiled coffee table with a large copper tub filled with fresh-cut blue and red anemones.

While she waited for him, Laura wandered over to the doors. In the twilight, the terraced garden below the villa had taken on a surreal beauty.

"When your grandmother came to visit, she used to stand right there with that same expression on her face. She had several interests, especially gardening. Do you also have a green thumb, as you Americans say?"

He was good at making small talk. She needed to try, too. "I don't know." Laura had been studious in her growing-up years so she could go into her grandfather's hotel business. It had been a man's world then. Still was, in many ways. She had to work hard to make her mark, and spent a lot of time in the office. That's where she'd met Adam, who was determined to rise to the top echelons of the company. They had that in common.

This trip to France hadn't been on her agenda, but she'd seized at the opportunity to learn more about her grandmother. Laura had put her assistant in charge while she was gone, satisfied he could handle things for the few days she'd intended to be away.

She turned in Nic's direction, bursting with questions. He was silent on several subjects, including his wife, but she needed to remember his personal life was his own. She felt his distrust, no doubt as great as her own. They were walking through a minefield, but especially after her rudeness to him in San Francisco, she had no right to expect information that was none of her business.

"Was that your grandfather on the phone?"

He nodded. "Maurice is coming now."

CHAPTER TWO

LAURA SWALLOWED HARD. The man she'd been taught to hate would be here soon. What was the real truth about him and his affair with her grandmother? No one was all black or white. The muscles in her stomach started to clench with anxiety.

"The château in La Colle is only ten minutes away. Please help yourself to coffee while we wait."

She sat across from Nic and sipped hers. "The word *château* conjures up images. Does it look like one of the Châteaux de La Loire?"

Nic eyed her over the rim of his cup with a bemused expression. "Would you believe me if I told you that when Maurice took her there for the first time, Irene thought he'd brought her to the château where Cinderella was born?"

This was the first time the man had allowed

her to see behind that facade of suspicion. Laura couldn't help but smile. "You made that up."

He sat forward to reach for a cookie. One black brow lifted. "Ask my grandfather." In the next breath he got up from the couch and walked into hall. When he returned, he handed her a five-by-seven photo in an antique frame, one she'd seen hanging among the others. "This is what the estate looks like. Hopefully it will satisfy your curiosity."

With this picture he'd just extended an olive branch of sorts. Even if he wished his grandfather hadn't put him in this position, she would take him up on it in order to uncover the truth. Nic had actually brought her to his home. She couldn't have imagined it when they'd first met in California.

"Maurice said Irene lived for the day when you would come to visit and she would take you through it room by room, because you loved castles and princesses."

"That's true. I can't believe she remembered that."

He studied her for a moment, as if weighing

her words. "Apparently you were taken with Cinderella, whose mean-spirited stepsisters had been cruel to her and made her sleep in the attic with the rats."

"She told you all that? I do have a terrible aversion to rats. A married friend of mine has a little boy who loved the movie *Ratatouille.* I start to watch it with them, but I couldn—" She suddenly stopped talking. Good grief. She was babbling.

His mouth broke into the first genuine smile he'd given her. That's when she realized how fabulous *he* was. Probably the most incredible looking and acting man she'd ever seen in her life. Laura had never met anyone remotely like him. Everything he said and did was starting to slide beneath her skin to draw her in. His wife had to be the luckiest of women.

Laura quickly looked down at the picture, only to cry out in wonder. After studying it, she lifted her eyes to him. "It *does* look like some of the pictures in my old fairy-tale book, the one my nana used to read to me. Your family home is beyond fabulous, Nic!"

"My great-grandfather Clement had the seventeenth-century château fully restored. He needed a lot of bedrooms and bathrooms so he could entertain business associates. There's an original baronial-style fireplace, stone spiral staircases and an enviable wine cellar. The conical roof and spring-fed moat add the perfect ambience."

"This is too much," she cried softly. To think her grandmother had lived there for twenty-one years. "Did you love the château, too?"

"*Bien sûr.* My parents lived nearby. The whole Valfort clan congregated there whenever possible."

"You must have had the time of your life!"

His smile slowly faded, letting her know his family had been in hell, too. That solemn pewter gaze of his traveled over her as if he were trying to figure her out. He had no idea that it sent an unwanted rush of guilty heat through her body. Heaven help her, but she was enjoying Nic too much in his wife's absence. This had to stop.

All the talk about her grandmother having had

an affair with Nic's grandfather while she was still married to her first husband had horrified Laura for years. She couldn't imagine getting involved with a married man. What would possess a woman to do that no matter how tempted?

Yet here she was feeling an attraction to this man who'd grown up disliking her and her family with the same disdain Laura had felt for his family. Was this how it had started with her grandmother? An attraction that eventually led to an addiction and in the end the two of them had thrown both families aside in order to be together?

One thing Laura did know. She shouldn't be alone in this house with Nic any longer than necessary. Without realizing it, Laura pressed the photo to her chest, reminding herself that the only reason she was here was because of Irene. Not because of Maurice's grandson, who was proving to be a disturbing distraction.

In a mournful tone she murmured, "My grandmother lived here all these years, yet I never once saw her after she married and moved away."

Nic stood there with his powerful legs slightly apart, his hands on his hips in a male stance. "I heard many versions of the Holden-Valfort saga from my own relatives before I was grown up enough for my grandfather to sit me down and tell me the unvarnished truth about their situation."

She lifted tormented eyes to him. "You condoned his version, whatever it was?"

Nic pursed his lips. "I love my grandfather without qualification. But I'd like to hear your version, if you're willing to tell me. We'll see if they match."

She put the photo down on the table and got to her feet. "My grandmother disappeared from my life when I was six. I have a vague memory of her, but I know most of what I know from my aunt Susan, Mother's elder sister, who has never married. She said that my grandmother had an affair with your grandfather even though his wife was still alive."

"That would have been impossible!" Nic bit out.

"I'm just repeating what I was told. All this

happened while my grandfather was battling cancer. Grandfather Richard died too young. Soon after his death, Maurice's wife died, so he married my grandmother and they moved to France. Neither Susan nor my mother could ever forgive Irene for having an affair while their father was so ill."

Nic's face had darkened with lines, making her nervous to go on.

"They said your grandfather was an evil man whose ability to seduce her while his wife was still alive created the scandal. They told her to get out of their lives and never come back.

"When I grew old enough to understand what adultery meant, I could see why Mother and Aunt Susan had been so devastated. When I was told the truth, the bitter side of Mother's nature came out. Our home was not a happy one.

"But over the years I've learned that no one is perfect and everyone makes mistakes. To remain so angry at my grandmother was wrong, no matter what she or your grandfather did. I told her I wanted to go see Irene. She forbade it.

"That's when I suggested she get professional

help, but she accused me of turning on her. It was awful. Every time I tried to reason with Mother, she'd shut me out and accuse me of not loving her.

"I made things worse when I tried to talk to my aunt Susan. She told me that if I ever attempted to get in touch with my grandmother, my mother wouldn't be able to handle it and it could push her over the edge."

The forbidding expression on Nic's arresting face filled her with alarm. He moved closer. "That story is so wrong and twisted, it'll tear my grandfather apart when he hears it." To her shock he clasped her upper arms, drawing her to his hard muscled body. His intensity was a revelation. "Maurice is euphoric you're here. Promise me you won't tell him what you just told me." A vein stood out in his neck. "Not yet, anyway."

"I—I won't say anything," she stammered. Her silence on the subject appeared of the most supreme importance to him.

His energy drove through to her soul. He was close enough she felt the warmth of his breath on her lips. When she looked up, his dark gray eyes were pinpoints of pain. "Why did you really fly here?" he ground out. "Was the lure of the will so great, you had to find out what amount of money she left for you? Tell me the truth." He gently shook her. "I can take it, but my grandfather can't!"

She was devastated by his reaction. "I guess I'm not surprised by your accusation. Because of the hate on both sides, it appears you really don't know one very important detail."

"What's that?" he demanded.

"My grandfather Richard left millions to our family—to *me,* personally. I've never wanted for money a day in my life and never will. The only thing I could never have was the joy of growing up around my grandmother. And though I'm loath to meet the man who took her away from us, I was determined to see what kind of man he is."

Her eyes flashed with pain. "What kind of power does your grandfather wield to be able to entice her to give up her whole life in California and come live with him in France? She didn't need money. My grandfather gave her everything!" Laura could tell her voice had risen. "Does that answer your question?"

A groaning sound came out of him.

"*Mon Dieu,*" he whispered, sounding utterly desolate. His hands slowly slid down her arms. But when he released her, she wasn't ready. Her legs felt so insubstantial she grabbed for the wing-back chair so she wouldn't fall.

While Laura was trying to recover from being held that close to him, she heard voices coming from the foyer. A woman and a man, both speaking French.

Shaken by the sound, she turned around and saw Nic's housekeeper usher in Irene's silver-haired husband from the photograph. He was dressed in a royal-blue sweater and cream-colored trousers.

In person he seemed young in demeanor for an eighty-one-year-old man whose face showed signs of recent grief. He was remarkably handsome and had passed on those genes to his grandson. Twenty-one years ago Laura's grandmother had no doubt been swept right off her feet.

He crossed the room, staring at Laura with incredulity before he turned to Nic. "You must have seen it the minute you met her." His French accent was more pronounced than Nic's.

"*Oui, Gran'père.* Laura is most definitely Irene's granddaughter."

Maurice's brown eyes swam with tears as they centered on Laura. "What she would have given to walk in this room and see you standing here! You're *ravissante,* just like she was."

From the first instant, all Laura could feel was love and warmth emanating from him. Though he and Irene had caused indescribable pain to her family, he couldn't possibly be the man her mother and aunt had demonized. She cleared her throat, still shaken by those moments when Nic had reached for her in pain. "We meet at last."

She had the sense he wanted to embrace her. Instead he held back and wept, pulling some tissues from his pocket. "It's a miracle. When she passed away, I thought my allotment had run out, but it isn't so. You've come. Please. Let's sit."

Once again she found a seat on one of the sofas. He sat next to Nic on the other. "How long have you been here?"

"I picked her up at the airport an hour ago," Nic explained. "She made a reservation at a hotel, but I canceled it."

She noticed Nic didn't mention the name. He wanted to shield his grandfather from the fact that she'd chosen *not* to stay at the world-famous Valfort in Old Town. Laura hadn't seen him do that. It must have been while she was looking at the photos in the hallway.

Maurice smiled. "*Naturellement.* You'll come to the château tonight. I'm all alone, rattling around in the place."

He wasn't the kind of man who rattled. Irene's husband seemed in excellent health. He was an exciting man, full of life and appeared athletic. She hadn't known what to expect. Certainly not this.

"That's very gracious of you, but I'd rather not impose when you weren't expecting me."

No matter how taken she was by him at first glance, Laura wasn't comfortable about accepting his hospitality. She wasn't comfortable with Nic, either, for several reasons, but she'd had no choice.

Nic must have sensed her distress, because he said, "Laura's staying with me tonight, *Gran'père*. The housekeeper has already made up one of the guest bedrooms for her. Tomorrow will be soon enough for the two of you to get better acquainted. Right now I believe she's exhausted after her flight. It's a long one across a continent and an ocean."

Laura's eyes met Nic's for a second. She felt he was trying to break up this meeting, in the kindest way possible, of course. Was he still afraid she might say something about the will? She was pained over his suspicions, but she understood them. There'd been so much ugliness between the families—this was the result. Could they ever trust each other?

She would have preferred to stay at a hotel. It would have been the wisest thing to do, but clearly Nic had wanted to warn her not to hurt his grandfather before she met him. Maurice nodded. "Of course. Did Nic give you those pictures?"

"Yes. I love them." Laura's mother had refused to look at them.

"Good. I took those during our many walks. We must have logged hundreds of miles throughout our marriage, exploring the countryside. She was a walker."

So was Laura.

The emotions Maurice evoked were choking her. "Nic told me you were very happy."

"We were soul mates. I adored her." His tears ran freely. "Up until the time she came down with pneumonia, we loved getting out every day together. No man could have been blessed with a better, more loving wife. I'm utterly lost without her."

Touched to the core by the sincerity of his love for Irene, Laura stirred restlessly. "How long was she ill?"

"Two months. She caught a cold. It developed into a secondary infection and before we knew it, she had pneumonia. Two weeks in the hospital on a regimen of strong antibiotics and the doctor was certain she would rally, thus the reason you weren't notified. But overnight she took a sudden, cruel turn for the worse and left this world quickly with one wish…that you and your family would know how terribly you were all loved."

Unable to prevent the tears, Laura got up from the couch and walked over to the French doors, too heartbroken to listen to any more tonight. Nic's words kept running through her mind: *That story is so wrong and twisted, it'll tear my grandfather apart when he hears it.*

After listening to Maurice's outpouring of love, she understood why Nic had asked her not to destroy this man while he was in mourning. This was no act, on Maurice's part or Nic's. She doubted she would ever repeat her version to his grandfather. There'd been enough suffering. Laura had lived an abnormal existence for years because of it. The bitterness in her household had tainted her life. She wanted no more of it.

"We'll get together tomorrow, *Gran'père.*"

At the sound of Nic's voice, Laura turned toward them. "Thank you for everything you've done, Mr. Valfort."

"Call me Maurice."

"All right then. Maurice it is." Moisture blurred her vision. "Thank you for sending Nic with my grandmother's body and arranging with the mortuary. In light of the history plaguing our families, it was a wonderful, noble thing to do. I'm indebted to both of you." Her voice caught.

His features sobered, showing his full years for the moment. "I must confess it was hard letting her body go." He broke down once more, clearly overcome with grief. "But I can always depend on my grandson to help me."

Her throat swelled, making it almost impossible to articulate. "He was very gracious." In light of the way she'd treated him, Nic was a saint. "Two days ago the family held a graveside service for her. She was buried in the family plot."

"Just as it should have been." The tears in his tone tore her apart. "But in return, *you're* here.

I thank God you came." His voice shook. "How she prayed for this day."

Laura felt the same way. "I wanted to meet you," she assured him in all honesty, but she just hadn't expected this feeling that he and her grandmother had been wronged in some tragic way. "She had to have loved you beyond anything."

"Not beyond anything," he contradicted her. "A day didn't go by that your name wasn't mentioned. She longed for her little granddaughter."

Laura couldn't take much more. Neither could Maurice, apparently. Nic put a comforting hand on his grandfather's heaving shoulder. "I'll walk you out."

She watched them go, but he didn't leave her long. When Nic returned, his middle-aged housekeeper was with him.

"I did that flight a week ago and it wiped me out. Arlette will bring you a light supper. Sleep as long as you want and we'll talk more in the morning."

"Thank you, but I don't think I could fall asleep yet. I need to relax. If you don't mind,

I'll call for a taxi to drive me into Nice." His head swerved in her direction. "I want to go down to the waterfront and soak in the atmosphere for a while. It will help me get a feel for the place where she lived all these years."

His chest rose and fell visibly. "Your grandmother used to walk along the Promenade des Anglais with Maurice at night. They'd stop to listen to music from the mid-'60s at a local brasserie. The place features *chanteurs* who sing the songs Brel and Aznavour made famous." He rubbed the back of his neck absently. "I'm wideawake myself and will be happy to drive you."

"No, no. You've done enough. I won't stay out long. I'm used to being out at night in San Francisco. A half hour is all I crave."

His eyes narrowed on her features. "Are you refusing me because you can't forgive me for insinuating something about you that is patently untrue?"

No. She was refusing because he was a married man. But if she said that to him, he'd think she was a very unsophisticated, silly woman instead of an executive at Holden who did business with married men all the time.

"If I accept, are you going to accuse me of deciding to leave the villa so you'll feel obliged to take me?"

A half smile escaped Nic. "Maybe I'm using you so I can enjoy a little diversion before I call it a night."

His wife had to have an awfully good reason to be away. If Laura were his wife...but she had to stop her thoughts right there. "Then I won't say no to your chivalry."

"I never expected to hear that particular word fall from your lips."

Her brows lifted. "I never expected you would willingly accompany me anywhere."

His chuckle followed her down the hall as she went to the bedroom for a sweater. He waited for her in the foyer and they walked out to his car.

Laura couldn't believe it, but they actually rode in companionable silence to the famous beachfront. Laura loved seeing the Promenade des Anglais, with its Italianate buildings, as portrayed in the many paintings of Nice. It ran parallel to the water. There was a magical feel about it.

He found a parking spot on a side street and they walked about a block and a half to the Oiseau Jaune. She could hear the music on their approach.

By some miracle Nic found them an empty bistro table among the crowd on the walkway and signaled a waiter. He ordered them mint tea.

Laura sat back, soaking up the authentic French atmosphere. "When I was in the Tetons of Wyoming last year, I went to a French restaurant in the mountains where they featured a singer who sounded like Charles Aznavour. This singer reminds me of him. I didn't understand the words, but I loved it. I have to admit, there's no place on earth like this. I can't believe I'm here."

"My grandfather can't believe you've come, either. I doubt he'll sleep until he sees you again tomorrow."

She fought tears. "To think I've missed this by staying away the whole time."

He angled a glance at her. "You were a victim of circumstances. That's what we've all been."

Laura took a deep breath. "I appreciate you bringing to this particular brasserie. For as long as I can remember, I've adored the sound and feel of this kind of music. You know, an accordion, a violin. Maybe a clarinet. It's *so* French. There's something about the tunes in your language that bypass conscious thought and find the romantic in you. But I do wish I knew French to get the full effect."

"You're Irene's granddaughter, all right. She had romance in her soul, too, and loved this place."

"That's nice to hear."

"I'll translate for you."

She glanced at him. "Please. I'd love to know what he's saying."

Nic's eyes were veiled. "'Let's dance the old-fashioned way, my love. I want you to stay in my arms, skin against skin. Let me feel your heart, don't let any air in. Come close where you belong. Let's hear our secret song and dance in the old-fashioned way. Won't you stay in my arms?

We'll discover higher highs we never knew before, if we just close our eyes and dance around the floor. It makes me love you more.'"

Oh...oh... Trembling, Laura looked away, spellbound by the words, by the way he said them, by his Gallic male beauty. She'd never known such a moment, such a night.

After twenty minutes the singer took a break. Laura smiled at Nic. "This was wonderful." Her voice shook. "I feel I'm really in France now and think I can sleep. How about you?"

"You've given me a new appreciation for one of my country's greatest assets. If your San Francisco legs are ready, I'll take you on a walk up to Castle Hill before going home. We won't go up all the way, but there's a wonderful view of Port Lympia to the east that's quite magical this time of night."

"Tell me about this place," she murmured. Anything to hear his deep voice speak English with that wonderful French accent.

"Castle Hill juts out a bit, like the Acropolis in Athens, but much greener, of course. It was named for a fortified castle and was redeveloped by King Charles-Felix of Savoy in the 1830s because of its amazing view. He added a landscaped park and an artificial waterfall."

Laura decided she'd been whisked away to a different universe as they climbed a ways above Nice. The music and the words had seeped into her bloodstream, where they would stay. To be out walking in such spectacular surroundings with this man was her idea of heaven.

She looked out at the sea. The romantic night called to her. Maurice had said he and her grandmother had walked hundreds of miles together. Now that she was in the South of France, she longed to see its wonders and clear her head. To see it with Nic left her breathless.

Eventually they returned to his car, but inside she rebelled that any of this had to end.

Wrapped in the beauty of the night, she closed her eyes and rested her head against the window during the drive back to the villa. Laura couldn't relate to the woman who'd flown to Nice earlier.

A change had come over her. Nothing was as she'd thought. Everything was different. The lines weren't clear anymore. She was terrified of what was happening to her.

The next day Nic was sitting at the dining room table reading the newspaper without absorbing any of it. He was troubled that he'd offered to drive Laura down to the waterfront last night. What had possessed him to take her walking afterward?

He couldn't understand himself. His family would *never* understand. If any of them had seen him with another woman while he was still waiting for word about his wife, it would shock them in a cruel way. But to know he'd been with the enemy when they didn't know she'd even come to France…

Ciel. What was wrong with him? Why had he done it?

Nic put down his coffee, crushed by guilt. Apart from Arlette and Jean, who lived in the back, Laura was the only person to have slept in his house since Dorine had gone missing. He'd let her stay here because he knew it was what his grandfather wanted.

And because you were trying to uncover her true agenda. Look how that turned out for you, Valfort!

He heard footsteps and lifted his dark head. Every time he saw Irene's granddaughter, she looked sensational. Yet beneath the surface he sensed her struggle over a situation that had plagued all of them for years. He discovered his own emotions churning. Today she'd dressed in chocolate-colored linen pants and a café au lait–toned blouse with a chic mandarin collar. She'd fastened her hair back with a tortoiseshell comb.

He got to his feet. *"Bonjour,* Laura."

"Bonjour," she mimicked him before putting up her hands. "Don't laugh. I only took Spanish and never could get the hang of the accent to my teacher's satisfaction."

Nic chuckled as he pulled out a chair for her. "Join me for brunch."

"Thank you. This looks delicious. I'm sorry I slept so late. The fabulous walk after the music last night lulled me into a deep sleep."

"No apology needed after that long flight." He saw signs she'd been crying.

She sat down and took a serving of quiche and fresh fruit. "How did my grandmother do in the accent department?"

"Exactly like you in the beginning. But she worked hard at it. Within two years she sounded French."

"So it *is* possible."

"Of course."

"There is no 'of course' about it. I work with people who've been in the States for years and they still sound like they came from somewhere else."

"An accent is something you have to cultivate. But in truth, your grandmother had an excellent ear."

"Being married to Maurice, she was no doubt motivated," Laura quipped. "It's evident he's an exceptional man. He couldn't have been kinder to me last night. I hope I didn't hurt his feelings by not accepting his invitation to stay at the château."

"My grandfather made the gesture in hope, but I interceded to give you time to adjust."

"I know, and I'm very grateful. For what it's

worth, I apologize for the way I treated you in San Francisco. Or maybe I should say, the way I didn't treat you. You were sent into a hornet's nest.

"Given the lovely evening out you showed this tourist last night, I should have taken you to some special spots in San Francisco. We could have eaten at my favorite restaurant at Fisherman's Wharf, ridden a trolley, driven up to Twin Peaks for the greatest view. Forgive me for being incredibly rude when you were only carrying out your grandfather's wishes."

"Just as you were holding up your end to the best of your ability," he inserted.

Now that Nic was getting to know Laura, he'd been forced to alter all his old concepts about her. With the gloves off, this woman was showing the perception and human insight she shared with her grandmother. It took that kind of depth to have attracted his grandfather. In truth, it attracted him.

He couldn't believe that in so short a time Laura had stirred up feelings inside of him without any design on her part. How had Nic allowed himself to get in this position when her family had wronged his over several decades? Since he was in love with Dorine and always would be, neither Dorine's nor Nic's family would be able to understand him having a desire to be with another woman. But for it to be *Laura?*

Their shock if they knew she was his house-guest filled him with despair. He would never want to let his family down, or Dorine's, but Laura's presence beneath his roof was impor-tant to Maurice. Unfortunately, no matter how pure Nic's intentions, their disapproval would pour down on his head once they found out.

"To be honest, I'm ashamed of my behavior," she confessed.

"No more than I. Yet we've survived our second skirmish intact. Are you ready for the third?"

Her inquisitive gaze darted to his. "Do I take it you've already talked to Maurice this morn-ing?"

Nic nodded. "He and your grandmother were early birds. Naturally he would like to come over. How do you feel about that? No one else will be here to disturb us."

She wiped her mouth with a napkin. "Please tell him to come. Will someone drive him?"

"Not my grandfather. He says driving is his one pleasure at this point and he refuses to give it up."

"It must be so hard to find himself alone. To have lived with someone all those years...I can't imagine it."

"To be sure, he's struggling. He's also apprehensive of your true feelings."

She bit her lip. "Whatever the problem with my family, I wasn't a part of it except to feel the fallout. You have no idea how eager I am to talk to him."

That would thrill Maurice no end. *"Bon."* He pulled out his cell phone and rang his grandfather to give him the go-ahead. The older man sounded elated before they hung up.

"Nic? Does your family know I'm in Nice?"

"Not yet. For the time being this meeting is just between the three of us. My grandfather is aware this is new ground for all of us."

Those lovely blue eyes were filled with anxiety. "Is the animosity as bad on your family's side?"

Time to tell the truth. "To this day none of his siblings or my parents or my aunts and uncles have approved of Maurice's second marriage. They couldn't very well banish Irene from the family, but they kept their distance so that she always felt like an outsider—except with Maurice, of course."

"And you."

He nodded.

"That means all of you have been in pain, like my family. How tragic," she whispered.

"*Tragic* is the right word. They thought my grandmother Fleurette was perfect. I did, too. At the end she suffered from a severe case of arthritis that deformed her extremities and kept her bedridden.

"My grandfather waited on her with such devotion and grieved for her so terribly, none of us thought he would ever get over his loss. When he announced he was getting married again less than two years after the funeral, it was hard on the family to comprehend."

"Two years?"

"Yes."

"But I thought—"

"I'm afraid you don't have all the information," he muttered gloomily. "There've been huge lapses of the truth on both sides of the Atlantic."

A distressed sound escaped her throat. "Whatever the truth, both sides of our families have suffered a lot of grief that I find appalling."

"You're not alone on that score. My family would have understood his finding a woman—or several women—to be with. But to actually get married again to a woman from another culture and bring her to the family home to live was a particularly bitter pill to swallow. It turned out she was the widow of Richard Holden, another hotelier who'd put Holden Hotels on the map in California."

Nic sat forward. "Did you know your grandparents and mine met at several world conferences with other hoteliers while they were in business?"

"What?" she cried.

"It seems the four of them struck up a friendship and did a little traveling together."

Aghast, Laura shook her head. "I didn't know about the travel."

"I'm not surprised. As they say, the devil is in the details, and you weren't privy to them. Maurice was saddened when he learned Richard was dying of cancer and visited their home several times before he passed away."

"Was your grandmother still alive at that time?"

"*Mais oui.* She went to Richard's home with him."

"So the idea of an adulterous relationship—"

"Is preposterous," Nic concluded for her. "It was two years later before arthritis turned on Fleurette and put her to bed. After her death my grandfather finally rallied and started working all hours. A year later there was an international conference in New York where several hoteliers were being honored. He discovered Irene was there to receive an award posthumously for Richard."

"So *that's* how they met again."

He nodded. "I leave it to your imagination to figure out what happened. Two strong people who'd been friends earlier and had a great capacity to love discovered they wanted more and fell in love."

Laura was fighting her emotions. "What a romantic story."

"Yes. My grandfather flew to California constantly to be with her. He tried to get to know your mother and aunt, but it wasn't meant to be. When he proposed, she said yes and they got married."

"Where?"

"In California. They had a private civil ceremony performed by a justice of the peace. He planned to settle there with her so she wouldn't have to be uprooted from your family. They could travel back and forth to France. Maurice had decided to install his brother, Auguste, to be in charge of the corporation while he consulted from a distance. But it wasn't meant to be, at which point Maurice brought her to France. He'll fill you in on the details."

"Their marriage shouldn't have decimated both families," Laura cried softly. "What's wrong with all of them?"

He shook his head. "I was twelve at the time. After hearing the family talk, I wasn't prepared to like your grandmother, who was taking the place of my *minou,* but that changed when he brought Irene to Nice to live and I met her. She was one of the most charming women I ever met, and it was clear to anyone they made each other happy. She became my unofficial English tutor."

Those blue eyes lit up. "Really?"

"We both enjoyed our informal sessions."

"You helped each other."

"Yes. As I grew older I heard the word *opportunist* in regard to her come up in hushed conversations at family gatherings. But that was absurd, since Grandfather told me she had plenty of her own money."

Laura pushed away from the table and stood up. "I don't understand any of it, particularly not the lie or the depth of my mother's and aunt's venom. After what you've told me, it doesn't make sense."

"I agree there's a big piece missing and had hoped you could enlighten me. Perhaps my grandfather will be able to shed some more light on the subject. Would you like to go down to the garden while we wait?"

"I'd love it. I'll get my sweater."

She joined him in another minute wearing a white cardigan. He opened the French doors onto the patio. From there he led her down stone steps to the garden.

"You'd never know it was winter here. Look at that exquisite array of flowers! Everything from pink to red and purple. No wonder they call Provence God's garden."

Her comment shouldn't have pleased him so much. "I don't pretend to know their names," he murmured. "I leave that to the gardener. Your grandmother could tell you about each variety. I do know she loved the patch of white narcissus over in the corner surrounding the Etruscan urn."

"They look like drops of snow in the greenery."

Nic moved closer, drawn to her in ways he couldn't explain. "Would you believe me if I told you Irene once said the same thing? Besides your looks, you two are uncannily alike."

He saw her shiver, but it wasn't that cold out. "If you want to know, it spooks me a little."

"Surely *spooked* isn't the right word—"

She avoided his eyes. "No one ever commented that my mother and I are alike. I guess my grandmother's genes were passed on to me. It's so strange to hear about how much we have in common when she was absent almost the whole of my life."

Nic found the similarities astonishing. Laura was so—heaven forgive him—alluring, even though he loved Dorine with all his heart. "There are differences, too, of course. Irene claimed to have no interest or head for business. You, on the other hand, hold the impressive title of marketing manager at Holden headquarters. Which means you inherited some of your grandfather Richard Holden's genius. I'm impressed. Maurice held him in great esteem."

His comment caused her to look at him through veiled eyes. "I keep learning things I didn't know. Tell me something else. How come you're not running Valfort Hotels?"

"That's all in the hands of family—my father, uncles, siblings and cousins. Maurice and his brothers watch over everything."

She cocked her blond head. "You're the dark horse. What do you do for a living?"

He'd wondered when she'd get around to asking him. Pretty soon she would want to know about his absent wife and he would have to explain. But he preferred not to tell her about Dorine while they were dealing with Laura's reason for coming to France. There'd be time enough later for that horrific, ongoing chapter in his life.

"I run my own research-and-development business in the technology park near here. My division deals with specialized information in life and environmental science, including fine chemicals. The park consists of eight competitiveness clusters. In layman's terms, we reinforce synergy between academic research and business through technology partnerships."

"Already you've more or less lost me," Laura said on a gentle laugh, igniting his senses that had been in a deep sleep. He didn't want to be awakened, particularly not by this woman. His family had never been able to accept Irene. Now her granddaughter had come, and the chemistry between the two of them was coming alive, but it just wasn't possible. His guilt was crushing him. "Sounds like the furthest thing from the hotel business one can get."

"I always liked the sciences and went to study in Paris, but my brother and brother-in-law are steeped in the hotel business."

"Yet your grandfather leans on you for everything of the greatest significance in his life."

She had his attention. "Why do you say that?"

"He said himself last night that he can always depend on you. Plus there's a feeling I sense between the two of you. You're strong like he is, or he wouldn't have sent you on a desperate mission that would have struck fear in anyone else."

Her remarks were so on target, they caught him off guard.

"Nicholas?"

CHAPTER THREE

THEY BOTH TURNED at the same time to see Maurice descending the steps, this time wearing his favorite leisure suit and turtleneck. His searching brown eyes darted from one to the other as he approached.

Because Nic bore a strong resemblance to his grandfather, he wondered if Maurice was seeing himself and Irene as they might have looked fifty-odd years ago, long before the two of them had even met. It raised the hairs on the back of his neck to consider the complexity of their incredibly unique situation.

This time Maurice kissed Laura on both cheeks. Their interaction seemed natural. "I'm sure Nic told you that your grandmother left something for you, otherwise you wouldn't have come all this way."

"That's not true!"

He glanced at Nic in query.

"Maurice, if my grandmother left me something, that thrills me, but I didn't come all this way because of a will. I didn't want the silence between our two families to last any longer. I wanted to talk and meet with the man she'd loved all these years. Not even my family could stop me. I've already told Nic this and hope you believe me."

He reached out to clasp her hand. "What you've just said is an answer to my prayer. Now I want to fulfill my wife's wishes. I spoke on the phone with my attorney, *ma chère*. He told me to go ahead and read the will to you. I could do that, but I'd rather show you. Why don't you come to the château around five?"

She nodded. "I'd like that."

"Good. I'll be waiting for you. In the meantime, I have things to do." He clapped a hand on Nic's arm. "I'll see you later."

"*Mais oui, Gran'père.* Let me walk you back to the car."

"No, no. Spend the time with Laura. Make her feel at home."

More guilt swept through him, but this was one time he had to fight it. When Maurice had disappeared inside, Nic turned to her. "What would you like to do in the next few hours?"

She looked all around her. "Nothing could equal the lovely evening last night, but I would like to do a little shopping in the Old Town I've heard so much about."

Nic would never forget last night either. He was haunted by his feelings. "The window kind, or do you have something specific in mind?"

"Specific for sure." She looked all around her. "Since Maurice couldn't bury my grandmother here, I'd like to do something in honor of their love. You say she loved flowers."

Nic nodded. "So did my grandfather."

"Then I'd like to take him some."

"Do you have a certain variety in mind?"

"No. Not yet."

"You'll have a worse time making a decision when I take you to the Marché aux Fleurs Cours Saleya."

Her eyes smiled. "What's that?"

"One of the most famous flower markets in

France. Grab what you need and we'll drive there."

Twenty minutes later he parked near the area with the pretty striped awnings. Beneath them she discovered thousands of flowers. "Nic—"

Their gazes met. "I know. Do you get the feeling they're making eyes at you?"

She laughed. "I do!"

They walked around for at least a half hour while she tried to take it all in. "Oh—I have no idea what to choose. It smells so heavenly here. Look at those geraniums!"

There was everything imaginable, from dahlias with their anemone-shaped flowers to vivid impatiens in glorious colors. But in the end he could see her attention was drawn to the mauve fuchsias. She stopped in front of the huge tub. "I think I have to have these."

The vendor spoke to Nic, who translated. "He wants to know how many you want."

"I wish I could have all of them, including everything in this market, but of course that's ridiculous."

"Not if this is your heart's desire."

In the next breath Nic said something to the man and handed him some bills from his wallet. The vendor grinned, then nodded to several of his workers. They picked up the tub and followed Nic to the car. He opened the trunk and they set it inside.

When the workers left, she looked up at Nic. "I don't know what to say," she whispered. Before he could take his next breath, she raised on tiptoe and kissed his hard jaw. "Thank you for another memory I'll always cherish."

The feel of her lips shook him to the core. To throw off the sensation, he said, "Come on. I'm going to take you to Fenoccio's. It's an ice cream parlor that serves exotic varieties."

"Like what?" she asked as they walked along.

"Have you ever tasted ice cream with violets?"

"You're joking!"

But of course he wasn't. In a few minutes they were both sharing a small cup of it. The flavor was different and quite delicious.

"Around this corner is another treat you have to try."

They stopped at Lova's, where he fed her

socca, a big pancake cut up into little strips and covered in black pepper, then eaten with the fingers. When he fed her a strip, her lips brushed his fingers, sending another curl of delight through his body.

"Um…that's good! We have to stop feeding ourselves if Maurice is expecting us to eat dinner. I need to do one more errand and know the shop. We passed it a minute ago."

Nic checked his watch. "It's getting late. Tell you what, I'll go get the car. When you're ready, call me and I'll pick you up."

"Thank you." As he started to walk away, she called to him. "I've never had so much fun."

Nic had forgotten what fun was like. Yet overnight she'd transformed the black world he'd been living in.

Dorine…forgive me.

Laura knew this afternoon was the only one she would have with Nic. Her guilt weighed too heavily for this to go on.

She was here to get to know Maurice and tried to imagine what it was her grandmother had left her. Her excitement was tangible. But intermingled with those thoughts was a growing awareness of the married man who'd just left her. She found him so appealing, she was afraid.

Laura had been rubbing shoulders with married businessmen for years, some of them very attractive. But nothing like this had ever happened to her before.

Was this how her grandmother had felt when she'd first met Maurice? Breathless and aware of a male energy that invaded her body, filling it with shocking new sensations? Nic's deep voice penetrated so that even when she wasn't looking at him, her nervous system responded to a force beyond her understanding.

Tomorrow she'd arrange for a flight to San Francisco and put this man behind her. She'd come to France for answers about her grandmother. With nothing else to be resolved, she didn't dare remain under his roof after today. Her guilt had reached its zenith.

Adam had texted her this morning. She'd texted him back that she'd get in touch with him later when she had something concrete to tell him. In truth, she didn't feel like talking to him. Whether her mother was right about his agenda or not, it didn't matter.

Last night Nic Valfort had happened to her... today he'd happened to her again, only with more force.

Maurice's grandson had already made such a breathtaking assault on her life and senses, Laura was reeling. When she could feel this attraction to an unavailable, married man, it meant she couldn't possibly make a commitment elsewhere that was worth anything. Certainly it meant she hadn't met the right man yet.

The old part of Nice was like a lot of the medieval villages she'd seen throughout Europe. She was charmed by its narrow streets curving in irregular fashion between old buildings with their red-tiled roofs. The streets were packed with shops and shoppers still needing to buy gifts. She'd almost forgotten tonight was Christmas Eve, thus the reason for this errand.

She went in one of the wine shops she'd spotted earlier and bought a Riesling and a Pinot Gris for her hosts to thank them for their hospitality. She asked that the bottles be gift wrapped. While she was waiting, she pulled out her cell phone, but it rang before she could call Nic.

Her heart thudded when she saw his name on the caller ID. She clicked on. "Hello?"

"*Bon après-midi,* Laura. Are you ready for a ride home yet?"

She sucked in her breath. "Your timing is perfect."

"Where are you?"

"At Chappuis et Fils. Sorry I pronounced it wrong."

His chuckle wound its way through her body. "I still understood you and will be there in five minutes. I'm already in my car. Don't go anywhere else."

Laura smiled. "I can tell you're a married man." She'd brought it up on purpose, if only to remind herself. "No doubt you've had to chase after your wife many a time, but I'll make this easy on you and promise to stay put."

She didn't know what she expected to hear him say, but it wasn't the long silence that met her ears. "Nic? Are you still there?"

"Oui." Then she heard the click.

Her brows met in a frown. What had she said? Was he separated from his wife? Maybe in the middle of a divorce? Maybe that's why he hadn't spoken of her. She didn't know what to think.

The shopkeeper handed her a bag containing her two parcels. She thanked him and walked outside, but the excitement she'd felt when she'd first heard Nic's voice had evaporated after hearing his dampening one-word response. He'd hung up, leaving her hurt and baffled.

It wasn't long before she saw his car come alongside her. She hurried to get in and shut the door, lowering her shopping bag to the floor of the backseat. He wound his way through a couple of streets to a broader thoroughfare without saying anything. When they reached the main road, he headed in the direction of La Colle-sur-Loup.

His dark countenance unsettled her. Anxious over the tension radiating from him, she stared out the window, wondering what was going on inside him. "Are you okay? Is your grandfather all right?"

"Your presence has infused him with new purpose. You have no idea. He needed me for a while because he wants this visit to be perfect for you."

Nice as that was to hear, it didn't answer her question about Nic himself. They drove another five minutes before he pulled off the road to a gravel drive. A canopy of trees made the interior darker as they continued through the wooded property.

When they rounded a bend, he pulled to the side of the road and stopped the car. By now her heart was thudding in trepidation. He shut off the engine and turned his dark head toward her. "My wife went missing three years ago."

Laura's horrified gasp resonated in the car.

"I'm presuming Dorine is dead, perhaps from the very first day. I'll never know if it was foul play. Maybe a vendetta against me or my family. If she was attacked and is still alive, the chances of her having amnesia are statistically improbable. If she was kidnapped, there was never a ransom note. If she left me for another man, it's been three years and I've reconciled myself that she's not coming back. If she became ill and died or committed suicide, her body has never been fo—"

"Don't say any more," Laura begged him. Without conscious thought she put a trembling hand on his arm.

Nic glanced down at it. "I was rude to you on the phone. That's because I was angry at myself." He let out a sigh. "When you first asked me if she knew I was bringing you home to the villa, I should have told you about her then. But you were already dealing with the pain of your grandmother's death and I didn't want to add to your discomfort."

"It couldn't have done that—"

"Then you'd be among the rare few who don't believe I had anything to do with Dorine's disappearance."

Her eyes closed tightly for a minute. "The rare few being your number-one defenders, Maurice and Irene. I know what you're about to tell me. The spouse is always suspect. That holds true in every country."

"Yes," he said grimly. "In some circles I still

am the prime person of interest. The police turned my house and office inside out and upside down looking for her. The newspapers had a field day exploiting the Valfort name. Jack the Ripper didn't get as much notoriety as I did. My entire family was vetted with criminal relish."

"I—I can't imagine a situation more ghastly." Her voice shook. "You don't need to explain anything to me." She squeezed his wrist before letting him go. "I don't know how you've been holding your world together." He was in such a horrible situation she could hardly bear it.

"In my darkest hours it was Irene who told me not to lose hope. She'd been ostracized from your family and mine, but she wouldn't let me despair. She told me I could rise above the suspicions and that one day justice would prevail and I'd get my life back. Her prediction was something I've held on to. For her to be gone has left me without one of my anchors."

"Oh, Nic—" Tears gushed from Laura's eyes. "I'm mourning the fact that I never got to know her, but I'm so sorry for what her death has done to you and Maurice. It sounds like my grand-mother was a saint."

"There's no question about that."

Laura wiped her eyes with her hands. "What was Dorine doing the last time you knew her whereabouts?"

"She worked at one of the other companies in the technology park. On that particular day, she told the secretary she was leaving for lunch. We know she drove her car into Nice and parked on one of the streets near a favorite restaurant of hers. But the proprietor claimed she didn't eat there that day.

"I was at work, but had left for a business lunch in Nice, then returned. It was almost time to go home when I received a call from the sec-retary. She wanted to know if Dorine was with me, because she'd never come back from lunch. That's when the nightmare began."

Laura kneaded her hands in anguish. "And it's never ended for you."

"It has been torture, I admit. At first I was on tenterhooks, thinking she was still out there somewhere. For the last couple of years, I've felt she's dead, but…"

"But you've had no closure yet and your character has been unfairly impugned. I'm so sorry, I don't know what to say. There are no words to comfort you."

"Thanks for not trying." His voice grated. "That sounded horrible, didn't it?"

"No," she said in a wooden voice. "Just heartbreakingly honest."

"You have an amazing capacity to understand."

"I don't. I'm just trying to put myself in your place. Knowing you, you've done everything humanly possible to find her."

He nodded. "Both her family and mine dedicated their lives to finding out what happened to her. So has Lt. Thibault, the detective who believes in me and wants to solve this case. Yet having unlimited financial resources still hasn't produced one iota of evidence that she's alive or dead."

Vanished without a trace… There had to be

an answer someplace, but he didn't want to hear her say it.

"On top of your pain, you've been trying to help your grandfather in his grief." She swallowed hard. "I was terrible to you in San Francisco and wish I could take it all back. If only there were a way I could help you now."

Her sensitivity was yet another quality that made her exceptional. "By flying here you've made a new man of him. That in turn helps me."

"Then I'm glad I came." It was impossible to keep the tremor out of her voice.

"Maurice has planned that we eat first. Normally we dine later, but this is a special occasion. I hope you can pretend to be hungry. If I know him, he's asked the cook to prepare your grandmother's favorite meal."

Don't say any more or I'll break down. "I'll show him I'm starving."

"You're wonderful." He gave her a quick kiss on the cheek.

Her head was bowed. "I can't imagine food tasting good to you when that darling young wife of yours is still unaccounted for. I saw a picture of the two of you in the hall. I could cry buckets for you. How do you stay so strong?"

This time his hand reached out to cover hers. "One day at a time. Three years have passed. I've had to cope."

She nodded. "What kind of work was she in?"

"Chemical research. Our two companies had business dealings from time to time."

"So you met through your work?"

"In a roundabout way, yes."

"Was she brilliant?"

"Very. We both loved science and had that in common."

"Life isn't fair." Laura had trouble breathing normally. "I'll tell the man upstairs when I talk to him again."

"Laura..." He gripped her fingers a little tighter before relinquishing them. "We'd better go before Maurice starts to get worried."

She wiped her eyes. "That's the last thing we want him to do."

Once again they were on their way. After several more bends, the château she'd seen in the photograph appeared. "Oh, Nic—"

Laura had been to the some of the châteaux on the Loire a few hours away from Paris, where the kings of France had held court. This one peeking through the trees was reminiscent of them, but much smaller in size.

Enchanting was the only way to describe its soft yellow facade. The combination of the Mansard-styled roofing and the coned towers took her breath. Lights shone from the three floors of evenly spaced windows, with their tiny square panes of glass. The sight was more exquisite than any picture in a fairy tale.

Nic pulled up in front of the circular drive and got out to help her. Laura was so mesmerized, she didn't realize how entranced she was until he opened the door. When he touched her now, his warmth seeped right into her bones.

On a shaky breath she said, "Would you mind bringing that shopping bag in the back? There's something in it for your grandfather." For Nic, too, but he'd find out later.

A half smile broke the corner of his compelling mouth. "Didn't Omar Khayyam say something about a bottle of wine and thou? Grandfather's cup will be running over."

She smiled back. Besides being heartbroken for him, she was so smitten by this man she was afraid he could see it in her eyes. Together they approached the entrance. Nic opened the massive door. *"Gran'père?"*

"Come in, *mon fils.* I'm in the *petit salon.*"

Laura felt like a time traveler who'd just stepped into old-world France. Any second now D'Artagnan might appear. No doubt the hundreds of guests lucky enough to have been invited to the Valfort home over the years had entertained the same thought.

Nic walked her through the immense foyer to a small salon. A dining room table with a lace cloth and candles glowing from the candelabra was set for three. Maurice, dressed in a formal suit and tie, came around and reached for her hands.

"Welcome to my home, *ma chère.*" That was the second time he'd called her *my dear.*

"I'm very happy to be here."

"She brought you a gift." Nic reached in the

bag and brought out two bottles of wine. When he saw the tags, his gray eyes darted to Laura's in surprise. "You got one for me, too?"

Her heart jumped. "Tonight two bottles of wine and thou sounds better than one, don't you think?"

Their eyes held. In that breathless moment, she knew he sensed her attraction to him. Embarrassed and feeling horribly guilty about it, she took the Pinot Gris from him and handed it to Maurice. "Merry Christmas."

The older man's eyes glistened. "We'll open it and drink to Irene, who would have given anything to be here tonight. You can freshen up through those doors at the other end of the room first."

"Thank you."

Talk about a trip down memory lane... But these were Irene's memories. Through the kindness of Maurice and Nic, Laura was privileged to peek in on them for a little while.

A few minutes later she returned to find Nic had brought in the tub of fuchsias and had placed it in the corner. Maurice greeted her with another hug. "You remind me of Irene. She always wanted to buy every flower at the market. Thank you for remembering her this way."

They sat at the table while Maurice opened the bottle and poured them each a glass. "I'd like to make a toast."

Nic caught her eye, letting her know through a silent message that her gifts had made his grandfather incredibly happy.

"To the long-awaited reunion. May there be many more of them to come."

"Amen," Nic whispered.

Laura didn't know how she was going to get through this meal, knowing Nic's hopes for his long and happy marriage had been dashed in the most cruel way she could imagine. If that wasn't enough, he had to go on living with the knowledge that some people still viewed him as the person responsible for his wife's disappearance. It made this moment bittersweet. They touched glasses before she took a sip.

Maurice smiled at her before drinking some of his. "I haven't had a drink of good *Alsacien* wine in a long time. You have excellent taste, just like your grandmother." A maid came in to serve them. "I hope you'll enjoy the coq au vin. Irene would have eaten it every night."

Laura's body broke out in gooseflesh. Too many coincidences. Her favorite meal at the Fleur de Lis in San Francisco was coq au vin. Nic had been watching her reaction and had probably read her thoughts correctly. He had the unusual capacity to see and feel beneath the surface.

"It's delicious, Maurice. Everything is perfect."

"Yet I see a new sadness in your eyes that wasn't there at noon. Why is that?"

While she was trying to find the words, Nic said, "I told her about Dorine."

"Ah. That explains it."

"I'm afraid it's my fault the subject came up." She explained what she'd said to Nic on the phone at the wine shop.

Maurice nodded. "In that regard you were right. Dorine loved to shop and often lost track of time, to the frustration of my punctual grandson. But that was a long time ago. Tonight let's put all the sadness away." *What else could they do?* "It's Christmas Eve and you're here. I'm going to read you the will right now and hope it will thrill you as much as it did Irene, who worked on your legacy for years."

My legacy? Laura frowned. "For years?"

"Twenty-one of them, in fact. She told me she took you to see the first Superman movie when you were six. When we got married and she came to live with me here, she grieved so terribly for her daughters and you, she decided to do what Jor-El did for the son he sent to Earth to be saved. You'll understand better what I mean in a minute."

Intrigued beyond words, Laura waited while Maurice pulled a paper from his pocket and unfolded it. He cleared his throat. "She made monetary provisions for your mother and aunt. Those provisions have already been sent to Holden headquarters by my attorney. But this provision is solely for you."

He looked down at the paper. "I, Irene Holden Valfort, being of sound mind and body, leave the summerhouse on the Valfort estate and everything in it to my darling granddaughter, Laura

Tate. It is hers for the rest of her natural life to do with as she pleases."

Laura felt dizzy and gripped the edge of the table. "My grandmother left me a house?"

"The one she and I lived in after we were married. She refused to stay at the château because it was where my life with Fleurette had been, and those memories were precious. So I restored the old summerhouse no one had used for a hundred years to make it livable for us.

"It was my wedding present to her. When she made out her will a few years ago, she told me she was leaving it to her granddaughter. She asked me that when the time came to go back to live in the château, because it would make my family happy."

"But who has lived in the château all this time?"

"Nic's parents, Andre and Jeanne, and my ailing brother, Auguste. His wife died a few years back. They've graciously allowed me to move in with them. Auguste and I love our card games."

"I couldn't take your home away from you!" Maurice put on a good front, but inside he had to be dying inside after losing her grandmother. Frantic, Laura's gaze swerved to Nic's. "I don't understand."

His gray eyes narrowed on her face. "You'll have to. It's legally yours."

Maurice got up from the table. "Come. Nic will drive us there and you can inspect it for yourself."

When she found the strength to stand, her legs—in fact her whole body—felt like jelly.

Nic drove them on the road leading behind the château and through the woods to a small lake. The summerhouse was half-hidden by a copse of oak trees. It had the same outer structure as the château, but had been built on a tiny scale in comparison. Laura fell instantly in love with it.

"Why is it called the summerhouse?"

"The head gardener lived there and used the rear of it for a greenhouse and nursery. The summer heat provided the perfect temperature for some of the exotic plants he cultivated."

"Nic told me my grandmother loved gardening."

"She became an expert."

Maurice helped her out of the car and walked her to the entrance. The front door opened to a small foyer that yielded a modern-looking, comfortable living room. The fire in the hearth sent up flames that flickered on the walls.

A handmade Christmas stocking with Laura's name hung from the mantel. In the corner was a decorated Christmas tree with twinkling lights. She breathed in the fresh pine scent. Nic must have come earlier in the morning to help get everything ready and put up the lights.

Dozens of wrapped presents had been placed beneath the tree. On one of the couches was a colorful throw made in blues and greens. A beam running below the vaulted ceiling held all kinds of intriguing-looking ceramics.

"Some of those gifts have been waiting years to be opened," Maurice explained. "Merry Christmas, Laura. This is the Christmas your grandmother has been working on for years. All of it for you."

Overcome by too much emotion, she broke down sobbing and buried her face in her hands.

* * *

The outpouring of grief, love and remorse coming from Laura was gut-wrenching. Three pairs of eyes were wet as Nic and his grandfather stared at each other. Nic was so moved he couldn't speak.

Maurice walked over and pulled Laura into his arms. The way she rested her head on his shoulder—like a young granddaughter might do—was a sight that would live with Nic all his life. It wasn't fair that they'd been denied this experience for so many years, but this Christmas had brought an end to the cycle of pain for Maurice. Nic was positive there could be a certain amount of healing for Laura now, too.

She finally lifted her head and kissed his cheek. "There are no words that could thank you for all this, Maurice."

"I don't need words. What I want you to do is sit down and watch a special DVD on the television set. Nic will turn it on for you. When it's over, there's a stack of them all labeled to watch. I'm going to take the car back to the château."

He looked at Nic. "Call me when you want me to come for you."

Nic handed his grandfather the keys. After Maurice left, Nic walked over to the TV set. "I haven't seen any of these videos. Maurice had them transferred to DVDs. Go ahead and make yourself comfortable. Your grandmother crocheted that afghan for you several years ago. Why don't you wrap yourself up in it?"

Wordlessly she pulled it around her and sat down on one end of the couch. She was so beautiful in profile, it was hard not to stare. Before he forgot why they were here, he started the DVD and joined her on the couch. Suddenly they were both seeing Irene after she'd become ill.

"I've left a lot of tapes for you, Laura, but this will be my last one. I feel it in these old bones.

"I never got to discuss the afterlife with you, but I know there is one and that one day you and I will meet again in person. But I can't leave this world without telling you one more time the joy it gave me when you were born. To be a

grandmother is a priceless experience for those women blessed enough to enjoy the privilege.

"As soon as you could make sounds, you called me Nana. You were the brightest, smartest, most adorable little girl on the planet. We laughed all the time. You were like a little golden angel from heaven. You loved stories, especially the Three Little Pigs. You were always so worried because they had to go out in the world without their mommy."

A sound between a laugh and a cry came from Laura.

"You had a sensitive heart at an early age and the most incredible imagination. You even made up voluminous stories of your own and drew pictures. I kept everything. You'll find them under the tree.

"Please do me a favor and don't be angry with your mother. She loved her father so much and believed that honoring his memory meant rejecting Maurice. But life's too short not to forgive, so forgive her for keeping us apart.

"You can experience a profound love more than once in this life, as Maurice and I found

out. Otherwise, what would be the point of existence?"

Those words jolted Nic to the quick. Possibly what Irene had said was true. But Nic couldn't imagine it. What if that second love came to an abrupt end, too? How did one bear the pain a second time?

"I was so lucky to have met two marvelous men. It hurts me that you never did get to know your grandfather Richard, who fell ill when you were so young. I'm hoping you'll get to know Maurice. To know him is to love him.

"He's a loving grandfather with half a dozen grandchildren. But I have to admit I've had a special spot in my heart for his Nicholas, who allowed me into his life when the other grandchildren weren't as open. I adored him and loved it when he came around. They are a lot alike. To this day he's been going through a great sorrow no one should have to go through in this life. I'm so thankful he and Maurice have each other.

"They're both in my prayers continually, as you are."

Nic sat there, moved to his very soul.

"I want you to know I love you and your mom and my Susie more than anything in the world. One day in the next life, we'll throw our arms around each other and all will be forgiven. For now, let me throw my arms around you through this video and the others I've had made over the years. Isn't technology a great thing?

"Enjoy this house—use it for a vacation or a place to come when you want to get away from the hotel business. I understand you show great promise in the marketing department and are destined to rise further with time. Good for you, my love. I often teased your grandfather Richard that behind every great man was a greater woman. I have no doubt that's you."

Laura smiled sadly.

"But whatever your future holds, promise me you'll let the grief of the past go. I've urged Nic to do the same. Be happy, my dearest grand-daughter. God bless you till we meet again."

The machine shut off.

"Oh, Nana—"

All Nic heard were the crackles coming from

the fireplace and Laura's sobs. She was bent over, utterly convulsed. Inwardly Nic was, too. He'd learned to love Irene and had never admired another woman more than he admired her. There was wisdom in that woman that defied description. Even in her outpourings to Laura, she hadn't forgotten Nic.

He got up and walked over to the beam to reach for one of the ceramic figures. "Irene bought a kiln and made her own crafts in the back room of the house overlooking the garden. She spent hours painting them. This is one I can remember her working on when I was just a young teenager. I thought it odd she'd chosen to make a pig. Now I understand. She'd obviously hoped to give it to you while you were little enough to appreciate it."

Laura took it from him. Through drenched eyes she examined it. Irene had painted Laura's name on the side. "This is so overwhelming. I can't take it in, Nic."

"Not yet, anyway. It'll require some time to go through everything."

She hugged it to her. "I don't know what to

do. Mother and Aunt Susan are spending Christmas together. I told them and Adam I'd be home Christmas night, but I can't leave yet. I—I don't want to." Her voice faltered.

The admission pleased Nic possibly too much, but when she dropped the man's name, his pleasure diminished. "Who's Adam?"

In the next breath she got up and put the pig on one of the side tables. "Adam Roth works in the accounts department at Holden headquarters."

"And?" he probed.

"We've been dating some."

Nic bit down hard. For a reason he didn't have time to examine right now, the news disturbed him. "Under the circumstances, he must be desolate you had to leave."

"He knows my grandmother's death has taken precedence over everything right now."

"Why didn't he come to France with you?"

"Because I didn't ask him," she said without hesitation. "This was something I needed to do alone."

Her response told Nic she couldn't be that deeply in love with Adam, or she would have wanted his support at a time like this. As for Nic, he would have insisted on going with her. Two people deeply in love should have no secrets.

She turned to him. "What I'd like to do is go back to your villa now and make some phone calls. They need to know I could be here for a while. Tomorrow I'll come back here and start going through everything."

"That's a good plan. I'll phone Maurice to bring the car."

CHAPTER FOUR

WHILE NIC CALLED his grandfather, Laura walked over to the tree and hunkered down to look at all the gifts. She reached for a packet the size of a postcard, curious to know what it contained. When she removed the paper, she discovered a dozen letters bundled together. They'd been mailed to her, but on the outside was stamped Return to Sender.

She scanned the dates and let out a horrified cry. These had been sent fifteen years ago. Laura started unwrapping the other presents that looked the same size. Before she was through, hundreds of unopened letters, some addressed to her mother and aunt, littered the Oriental rug.

"Laura?"

"Look at all these letters Nana wrote to us, Nic. Every one was sent back!" She got to her feet, almost hysterical. "How could Mother have done that?"

As she trembled in pain, he put his arms around her. She knew he was only trying to comfort her, but he'd chosen the wrong moment. In her vulnerability she fell apart against him. For a little while he simply cocooned her in place until she regained control. It felt so good…he smelled so good…

What are you doing, Laura? her conscience nagged at her. "I'm sorry," she said in a dull voice, and finally pulled away from him when it was the last thing she wanted to do. Her emotions were in chaos for too many reasons. "Forgive me for going to pieces like that. I'm so ashamed." She started gathering the letters, but he stopped her.

"Leave everything until tomorrow. Tonight you're emotionally exhausted. We'll come in the morning after breakfast and sort them. Let's be thankful your mother didn't destroy them. This way you'll have your grandmother's letters to read. Little slices of life you'll be able to savor."

Nic was wonderful beyond belief. She nodded

and looked at him. "You're right. I don't know how I'll be able to make this up to you and your grandfather, but I'm going to try."

Whatever he would have said was interrupted by his cell phone ringing. "He's here. Let's go."

She put one of the letters in her purse and took the afghan with her. Nic grabbed one of the DVDs and turned out all the lights. They left the house for the car, where they found Maurice sitting in the back.

On the short drive to the château, he said, "I'm aware this has been an emotional night for you, Laura. Go home and get a good sleep. We'll talk more tomorrow."

"Definitely. Thank you, more than you'll ever know, Maurice."

"I've only carried out your grandmother's wishes. Don't forget the bottle of wine for you, Nic. It's here in the back. *Bonne nuit.*" He patted both their shoulders before getting out. She watched him go inside the château before they drove away.

"I don't see a sign of anyone else around the château, Nic."

"No. When my parents learned you'd come, they went to my sister's for a few days to be with the other members of the family."

Laura was filled with fresh pain. "So the pariah from San Francisco descended, forcing them to leave."

"Never say that again!" he exploded.

"Do they know about Irene's will?"

"Not yet. Maurice will tell them soon enough."

"Nic—"

"I know what you're going to say, but let's not discuss it tonight."

"I have to. I can't live there and come and go from time to time with your parents close by." *I couldn't live in the same country where you are, Nic.*

"Maurice will be there."

"Of course! This estate and everything on it belongs to him and your family, including the summerhouse. He restored it to accommodate Irene's wishes, and, yes, it was their home together for a period of his life. But she's gone now and he should be able to embrace his whole family again."

"He does that."

"It wouldn't be the same with me around and you know it! Maurice ought to be able to spend time at the summerhouse and the château where everyone can congregate with no more outsiders. You know deep down I'm right."

She saw his hands tighten on the steering wheel. "Do me a favor and humor Maurice right now. He's made it possible for you to discover your grandmother. Let her message to you sink in. The rest will work itself out in time."

"No. It won't work itself out at all unless I take the proper steps to make things right."

He accelerated onto the main road, headed back to his house. "What steps?"

Her pulse picked up speed. "I realize my nana wanted to show me how much she loved me, but she didn't really expect me to keep the house."

"Say that again? You heard Maurice read her will."

"I also know that she refused to live at the château when Maurice took her there. There's no way I'm going to live on the estate. That would be the same thing." She turned to him.

"It was the gesture that counted, don't you see? But that's all it could be."

"Laura—"

"The day after Christmas I plan to hire an attorney here in Nice. I'll have him draw up the papers and will the house back to Maurice."

"You can't do that."

"Oh, yes, I can. That way your family will never know about my grandmother's will. I don't want them hurt. As for Maurice, it will be my gift to my step-grandfather for uniting me and Nana. But I'll make him the promise that we'll talk on the phone all the time and I'll come to visit him often."

She heard Nic's sharp intake of breath. "If you do that, he won't be able to handle it."

"That's your love for him talking. But remember that he's in the throes of grief, trying to hang on to Irene. She knew he'd suffer. That's why she willed the house to me. By doing so, he'd have something of hers to hang on to, through me. Admit I'm right."

He kept silent, but she knew he'd heard her.

The man was too intelligent not to know she was speaking the truth.

"Those two loved each other to distraction. It's so rare to see a love like that, with both of them trying to help the other. I'm so touched by it I could cry all over again. But it doesn't have to work that way now. I'm alive and I love him already. I swear I'll come to see him a lot. Our visits will keep her alive for both of us without the house to drive another wedge."

As for tomorrow, Laura planned to spend Christmas Day opening her presents and getting them packed to ship back to San Francisco. But by now Nic was silent in that scary way that broke her heart, because he was dealing with unresolved grief of his own. She decided not to tell him any more of her plans tonight.

By the time they reached the villa, the tension between them was palpable. After they went inside, he put the DVD on the table and unwrapped the bottle of wine she'd given him. He uncorked it and poured some into a couple of wineglasses.

"I think we could use a drink." So did she.

He handed her one before tasting it. "Thank you for this. I haven't enjoyed Riesling in years."

She took a sip. "Hmm. It *is* good."

They stood facing each other. "Need I remind you how guilt ridden Maurice has been all these years, keeping Irene away from her own family? He desperately wants to make it up to you. If you will the house back to him, it will be like a slap in the face."

"That's why I intend to have a long talk with him about guilt." Nic had said his grandfather might be able to shed some light on why Laura's mother and aunt had lied to her, but it was a talk she wanted to have with him in private.

"I don't think it will do any good."

"Maybe not, but after hearing my grandmother on the video, he has nothing to feel guilty about. You saw all those returned letters she wrote. Those two committed no sin just because they loved each other. My mom and aunt are the culprits here, no one else. They should be writhing in guilt for keeping everyone apart."

Nic's black brows furrowed. "He won't see it that way."

"He will after I point out the facts. Clearly Nana loved Maurice so much she went to France to live with him. He didn't haul her off at gunpoint."

At that remark, his lips twitched, letting her know he was listening. Nic was handsome in the way that hurt.

"She went willingly because she was compelled by her deepest feelings. A lesser love wouldn't have held her. A lesser love on his part wouldn't have stirred him to marry her."

He drank what was left in his glass, communicating his agreement without words.

"You said they were strong people, Nic. They were and are. It's my opinion that everyone on both sides of the ocean was intimidated by such a profound love in the beginning. But all of that could have been overcome if something evil hadn't happened."

"Evil?" His expression reflected surprise.

"Yes. I know you were right when you said a big piece of the puzzle is missing. My aunt used the word *evil* in reference to Maurice. How could he possibly be evil when Nana loved him so much? I've always been curious about that. Now that I'm armed with information I didn't have before, I'm going home to get the truth out of Aunt Susan and Mom. I'd like to liberate Maurice from the hell he's been in all these years."

She wanted to liberate Nic from his own wretched hell.

Putting his glass down, Nic reached out to cup the side of her face with his hand. He shouldn't be touching her. She shouldn't be letting him, but she couldn't move. The man would never stop missing his wife...and Laura wanted his touch too much. If anyone was evil, *she* was.

"You're a rare woman," he said in a husky voice.

"Because I want to get to the bottom of this mystery? I think not. As it is, I let it go too long." Struggling with all the willpower she possessed, she eased away, forcing his hand to drop. "What is it they say? Those who don't know their own history are doomed to repeat it? I never want to cause a repeat of what happened to our two families because of ignorance."

"Nor I."

She wandered over to the couch and sat down. "Nic? Before I go to bed, I want to ask you a question about something else not related to our grandparents."

He found himself a chair opposite her. "Go ahead."

"I haven't been able to get your wife's disappearance off my mind. Is there any new avenue I could help you pursue while I'm here? Do you want to brainstorm?"

Nic sat forward with his hands joined between his legs and shook his dark head. "That's a kind offer. Don't think I don't appreciate it, but I've been stuck for three years now."

"You said she drove her car to a street near her favorite restaurant."

"In the same block."

"Did she normally eat with friends?"

"Not often. Once in a while someone from out of town working on the same project would fly into Nice. They'd always eat at the Bonne Femme."

"Was her work classified?"

"Some of it."

"Where do those people live who were working with her at the time she disappeared?"

"She had several projects going. One team in India, the other in China."

"Did she travel to those countries?"

"Sometimes."

"Has the detective on her case learned of any deaths or disappearances of people in those countries associated with her company before or after she went missing?"

"Not that I've been told."

"Maybe she was the victim of a corporate espionage scheme and those countries have withheld information. It's possible she was lured away from her office by someone on the team she would never have suspected could do her harm. Did she have her laptop with her?"

His head reared. He stared hard at her. "Yes. She took it back and forth from the office." Nic got to his feet. "Where are all these questions coming from?"

She took a deep breath. "I work for a big corporation. When I go out for lunch, it's usually with a regional manager who flies in to talk business. It would never dawn on me that one of the hotel managers I routinely visit through-out the state would come looking for me to in-jure me. But if so, I would have no reason to be nervous when first approached."

He looked tired as he rubbed the back of his neck. She wished she hadn't said anything. "I'm sorry I brought up something so painful."

"No. I'm glad you did. It prompts me to call Lieutenant Thibault and run your thoughts by him. The French Sûreté has resources at Inter-pol that could find out if evidence from those countries to do with her firm has been sup-pressed over the last few years."

She got excited. "It wouldn't hurt." To be ex-cited sounded so awful, but if Nic could finally find out what happened to his wife, he could learn to live again. To get through each day *wasn't* living, not when certain fingers were still pointed at him. Her heart ached for him.

"You're right." His eyes played over her with a thoroughness that sent a tingling sensation through her body. "What do you say we do something happy and watch another DVD? I brought the one sitting on top of the stack."

"You just read my mind." They needed to get off painful subjects.

"We'll go in the den and watch on the big screen. I need a large one for my work. Bring your wineglass."

She reached for the afghan and did his bidding, following him into the next room on the other side of the house. One lamp was burning. No clutter in here. Just state-of-the-art equipment, bookcases with scientific tomes and some wonderful framed black-and-white photos of an eclipse of the moon in many stages. Riveting!

He poured more wine for them, then put the disk in the machine. The rounded couch filled one wall and part of the other. It was roomy and comfortable. A long, narrow coffee table was placed next to it.

Laura took off her shoes and sat on the end of the couch with her feet curled up under her, throwing the afghan over her.

Nic watched her. "Maurice used to hold the

skeins of yarn while Irene wound it into balls while she was working on that afghan for you."

"A labor of love," she mused aloud. "I would have given anything to see them together."

"Perhaps you will through the videos." Nic removed his suit jacket and tie. After unbuttoning his collar, he rolled up his sleeves to the elbow.

When he sat down, he extended his hard-muscled legs and crossed them at the ankles. She was far too conscious of his arms spread across the top of the cushions. His nearness filled her with unassuaged longings.

He glanced at her and sipped a little more wine. "This is nice. Maurice isn't the only one who's been rattling around in an empty house."

Nic.

Their eyes clung for a minute. "After all you've done and been through, I'm glad you're able to relax with me. Who would have thought it after our inauspicious beginning in San Francisco?"

His quick smile melted her bones. "That's what your coming has done for me."

She looked around. You have such a beautiful home."

"Dorine found it and decorated it."

Laura was surprised. "Where did you live before your marriage?"

"At an apartment in Nice she found uninspiring." Laura smiled. "I was so busy building my business, I didn't want to be a home owner, with all the headaches."

"But you took them on with her."

He nodded.

She should stop talking in case it was making his pain worse. "Shall we see what Irene wanted me to see?"

"The DVD case says this was filmed nineteen years ago."

"Nineteen?" she cried. It didn't seem possible.

Once again he smiled that devastating smile that caught at her heart. "You'd be eight, and I, fourteen. I confess I'm totally intrigued to find out what's on here." He pressed the remote.

In an instant there was her grandmother, big as life, but much younger, beautiful, dressed in pants and a blouse and standing against a hilly background. Would that Laura might look half that terrific at her age one day.

"Darling Laura, Maurice has brought me to the fortified city of Carcassonne, famous for the Crusades in 1209. One day you'll learn about them in school. My husband is taking the movie right now. You always loved palaces and castles. I thought you'd like to see this place. I wish you could be here. Maurice's grandson Nic has come with us. I call him Nic even though his name is Nicholas. The longer name is too formal.

"He's as fascinated by this place as I am. Come over here, Nic, so Laura can see what you look like."

A lean fourteen-year-old Nic, with longer hair, already getting tall, made a face for the camera. He appeared in a turtleneck and jeans, showing the promise of the breathtaking man he'd become one day. Laura jumped to her feet.

"Nic—that's you! Pause it for a minute! This is unreal. Do you remember that day?"

He chuckled and leaned forward. "Vaguely. Was I really that pathetic?"

"This movie is priceless. Press the remote again."

Pretty soon Irene took a picture of Maurice looking sporty in a windbreaker. His hair was still black and quite full, with only a few streaks of silver. Then Nic placed the video camera on a nearby ledge while he took a picture of the two of them. Maurice kissed Irene, hamming it up for the camera. They acted like teenagers. Laura heard Nic say, *"Oh, là là, Gran'père—"*

At this point both Laura and Nic collapsed with laughter. Laura had never enjoyed anything so much in her life. The teenage Nic larked around as they toured the battlements and fortifications. When the video came to an end, Laura made him play it again. She couldn't get enough. After the second run-through, he turned it off.

She darted him a glance. "Our grandparents left us both something precious, Nic. Now I know how Superman felt when he saw his father for the first time."

Nic's half smile made her legs shake.

"If Maurice didn't make another set of these

for himself, then I'll have them made for you. The first time I saw you with Maurice, I could tell there was an affinity between you. Now I know why. Did your parents make movies with you and your siblings?" She wanted to know anything and everything about him.

"A few. My father doesn't like to bother with a camera. Maurice calls him what would be the equivalent of 'sobersided' in English."

"My mom was more like that, too."

Much as Laura wanted to stay up all night with him and talk, she didn't dare. He had a wife who could be alive somewhere. *What do you think you're doing, Laura?* Her guilt was killing her. The more time she spent alone with Nic, the worse it was getting. She didn't even want to think about saying goodbye when the time came.

After thanking him for letting her see the video, she put the afghan over her arm and walked through the den into the living room. Nic was close behind her, making her go weak in the knees.

Laura picked up her purse from one of the

chairs. When she reached the hallway, she turned to him. "Good night, Nic. Thank you for the most wonderful day of my life. I have to believe a day is going to come in your life when you feel the same way."

Nic watched her disappear. For a while tonight he'd known a happiness he hadn't thought he'd feel again. He'd found himself concentrating on Irene. Being able to see Laura in her, the way they both laughed and got excited over everything, tripled his enjoyment.

It had been so marvelous sharing the video with her, he hadn't wanted it to end. Laura's arrival in Nice had brought Christmas back into his life.

But following those feelings came this excruciating attack of guilt. Nic buried his face in his hands. "Dorine, darling." He broke down sobbing. "I haven't given up on finding you. I haven't. Forgive me. Where are you? Please, God. Help me."

When he'd recovered, he texted the detective on his wife's case. Once he'd made the request prompted by Laura, he went back to his den to watch TV.

When he was next aware of his surroundings, it was morning. For the first time in ages he'd fallen asleep before going to his bedroom. To his surprise Laura's afghan had been thrown over him. That's why he'd felt warm—she had to have come in here again.

"Bonjour," Laura said in better French than before. He sat up to see her walk in the den carrying a tray with brioches, juice and coffee. She wore a navy T-shirt and jeans and was charmingly barefoot. "Stay where you are. It's Christmas morning and you deserve to be waited on."

She put the tray on the coffee table and handed him a mug of coffee. His attention was drawn to her fragrance and the blond hair she'd left long. It hung over one shoulder. "Arlette told me this is the way you like it—lots of sugar and cream. *Joyeux Noël!* Your housekeeper has been helping me with the pronunciation."

Ping went the guilt again for enjoying this moment with her. He was close to speechless.

"That sounded perfect. But you shouldn't be waiting on me when you're the guest."

"I think we've graduated beyond that point. I told Arlette we're family. After watching that film, I'd say you and I are the long lost grand-cousins of Atlantis or some mysterious forbidden continent like that, united at last."

She grabbed herself a mug. "Here I thought I'd sneak another look at the movie for my Christmas-morning treat. But lo and behold, I discovered Santa had arrived ahead of me, totally exhausted after his trip around the world spreading joy." Her laughing blue eyes traveled over him, warming him in new places.

He burst into laughter that resounded in the room. "If I snore, I don't want to know."

Her chuckle filtered to his insides. "I would never tell. But I must say you don't look a thing like *Père Noël*."

Nic rubbed his jaw, feeling the growth of his beard. "I don't remember the last time I slept in my clothes."

"That's good for you. I knew Santa had to be wearing something else beneath his red suit.

It means you were rid of tension for a change. You've managed to make me and your grandfather so happy, it's time someone did something for you. No one deserves happiness more than you," she murmured with an ache in her voice she couldn't disguise.

Everything Laura said and did was getting to him. What in the hell was he going to do about it? She handed him one of Arlette's Christmas rolls on a napkin. Then she took one for herself and sat down on the other end of the couch.

"When we left the summerhouse last night, I grabbed one of the letters from the floor that had been addressed to me specifically." She pulled it out of her pocket, and his eyes were drawn to the feminine curve of her hips. "Do you realize all these were handwritten? She had the kind of penmanship you don't see anymore. After I got in bed last night, I read it. You need to hear what it says."

Nic felt Laura's magic distill over him like a fine mist. He turned toward her, munching on his roll. He'd never felt so conflicted in his life.

All he could do right now was be happy for her. "I'm all ears."

"'My darling Laura, today Maurice and I will have been married ten years. We're in Venice. He's gone out to get a newspaper, but I know he left because he was upset and didn't want me to be aware of it.

"'The only shadow on our marriage has been the inability to share it with our loved ones. Today he got all broken up when he asked me if I'd been happy. A question like that is impossible to answer. He *knows* I've been blissfully happy with him, but deep inside he's not convinced.

"'Tonight he asked me if I wanted to leave him and go back to all of you. He believes that if we end the marriage, you will forgive me.'"

On a groan Nic sat forward, hurt for what the two of them had been forced to endure over the years. But he also groaned for the loss of Dorine, for the situation that had developed since Laura's arrival in Nice.

"'I've never seen him this upset before. Maurice blames himself for taking me away from you.

I don't understand it. I feel he's keeping something from me, but I don't know what it is.

"'No matter what I say, I can't talk reason with him. The truth is, your mother and Susie will never forgive me for loving a man other than their father. Without Maurice's knowledge, I've been seeing a therapist in Nice about our situation.'"

Nic grimaced. "Her pain had to have been exquisite."

Laura nodded with glistening eyes, then went on reading. "'He's a doctor of psychology. He said that my children's anger has its roots in something much deeper than their not wanting to accept my marriage. His advice is to confront my daughters openly.

"'I've tried that. They won't see me or accept my phone calls. Tonight I tried to get Maurice to open up and tell me why he feels so guilty. If he's holding something back, what is it? To my devastation, he left to do an errand. It breaks my heart.'"

Until now Nic hadn't realized that Maurice had felt such crippling guilt.

"'Forgive me for baring my soul to you, but you're a part of me. When I write to you, I can imagine us being together face-to-face. I need that. All my love, Nana.'"

Heartsick over their grandparents' pain, Nic got up from the couch. The joy of Christmas had been but a fleeting moment after all. The letter Laura just read had managed to darken the sky once more. Both men had lost the loves of their lives. Nic never wanted to open himself up to this kind of pain again. Maurice had lived through it twice. Nic couldn't.

He glanced down at her. That lovely face had taken on a sober cast. Her eyes searched his. "Do you believe Maurice knows something he was never able to tell Irene?"

"I don't know," he murmured, "but I'm going to find out, because this has gone on long enough."

She jumped up. "I'm so glad you said that. Let's confront him together with this letter. He needs to know Irene went to a therapist to try to help them. The two of them loved each other too much, always trying to shield the other from pain."

Nic rubbed his chest absently. "That's exactly what they did. Whatever secret still lurks, it robbed them of a lot of happiness."

Her features hardened. "It robbed everyone on both sides. Yet their love was so strong, they managed to survive it. That's what real love is all about. Nic…you and I have the power to turn things around."

He admired her courage more than he could say. "We'll do it." He finished off his orange juice. "After I've showered and changed, I'll drive us to the summerhouse. We'll open all the presents under the tree. Maurice will join us after he's spent time with the family. Then we'll talk to him about this letter."

"While you do that, I need to make those phone calls I forgot to do last night."

Being Christmas, naturally she'd ring her mother and Adam, the man who desired her. What man with a pulse wouldn't want her? But Nic couldn't be that man. He didn't want to be. He needed to find his wife.

"Laura?"

"Yes?" He heard the throb in her voice.

"Santa thanks you for Christmas breakfast. He hasn't had such a pleasant surprise in ages."

"It *was* fun before I spoiled it and read you the letter."

"I'm glad you did."

Her eyes clouded over. "I hope you mean that."

He meant it all right. With Laura on their grandparents' side, it added the kind of leverage needed to get the truth out of Maurice. Irene had suspected he hadn't told her everything. That woman's instincts couldn't be wrong. For twenty-one years they'd all been in a straitjacket. It was time to remove it.

Nic watched Laura reach for the afghan and leave the den ahead of him. Filled with a new sense of purpose, he found Arlette and asked her to prepare a basket of food for the three of them to enjoy at the summerhouse. With that accomplished, he showered and shaved, then put on trousers and a crewneck sweater.

Laura was ready and waiting for him in the living room, still dressed in the same outfit, but wearing sandals and her cardigan. He couldn't tell by her expression how her phone calls had gone, but if Nic were Adam, he would have taken the first plane to Nice and demanded to find out why she hadn't wanted him there. Didn't the man know not to take love for granted? It could be snatched from you in a minute, and Laura was a prize.

When they reached the car, he put the basket in the back and turned to her. "Isn't there a song in your country about over the river and through the woods?"

Her mouth broke into an enticing smile. "To grandmother's *petit* château we go," she sang, improvising as she went. "Clever Santa knows the way, in his dishy Mercedes sleigh, to avoid the ice and snow."

Nic grinned in spite of himself. He kept trying to control his feelings about her, but then she'd say something like that and his delight in her just kept growing. She had an amazing sense of humor that came out at the oddest times. A spontaneity so different from Dorine, who was a more controlled, structured kind of person.

In that moment he realized that the woman he'd once thought was the enemy had sung her way past his defenses and was close to— *Don't say it, Valfort.* He didn't want to, but his mind finished for him anyway. He feared she was reaching his stronghold.

They stepped inside the house, noticing that Maurice had sent some staff over to light another fire and turn on all the Christmas lights. But they hadn't touched anything else. The letters still lay scattered on the floor.

Nic put the basket on the table. "I'm going to hunt for some boxes. We'll sort the letters by date."

"I can't wait to read all of them."

"You have months of reading pleasure ahead of you, but I would wager you're anxious to open all the other packages first."

He heard her breath catch. "I admit it. I'm as bad as a child."

They worked together and soon the letters were neatly packed. Nic set them out of the way. "Now I'll play Santa and give the presents to you one at a time."

She knelt down next to him, her blue eyes shining in anticipation. In the video, Irene had painted an image of Laura at six years of age. Nic could almost see her as she'd been then. It clutched at his heart to think she'd been deprived of her grandmother all these years.

Each present had a tag with an explanation. Maurice and Irene had traveled a lot. Before long a series of gifts from around the world surrounded them, handpicked to bring Laura pleasure. Nic enjoyed witnessing her reactions.

She particularly loved the porcelain mask from Florence. But then the miniature Hans Brinker ice skates from Amsterdam thrilled her. Before long she was enraptured by the hand-carved music box from Vienna that played "Waltz of the Flowers." The last, from Egypt, was a hand-carved wooden Mary. She was holding the baby Jesus while Joseph led her on the donkey.

When the gifts came to an end, Laura shook her head. "This is too much."

"Twenty-one Christmases in one is a lot to take in," Nic murmured. "There's still more."

He handed her another gift, which turned out

to be a box. "What on earth?" She reached inside and pulled out dozens of sheets of artwork made by a child. "Nic," she virtually squealed. "She saved the drawings I made for her!"

Nic moved closer. Together they looked at each one, some large, some small, each paper filled with scenes of stick figures done in crayons and markers. There were several pictures of castles.

"Like Nana said, I was preoccupied with fairy tales. Oh, look—I've done pictures of the Three Little Pigs. My pigs are pathetic! I made the brick house go up to the very top of the page."

"You've drawn the wolf climbing up the wall. You didn't want him to get the pig," he teased.

"This is incredible. Look—I made my *L* backward in my name. The *A* looks like a snail."

More laughter ensued from both of them.

"But you turned it around in the pictures at the bottom of the stack," Nic pointed out. "These latest ones are very revealing. Do you see what I see?"

She nodded. "I've drawn me and my mother and father. But I also included my nana and grandfather. It has to be Nana because I put blond hair on her and brown on Mom."

"You printed her name above her head."

"The *N*s are sideways and look like *Z*s."

"I see you drew glasses on your grandfather and made his hair brown. He's shorter than your father here. You put black hair on him."

"My grandfather was only five foot nine. Dad was six feet. Daddy—" she whispered as a pang of remembrance hit her. "I loved him so much. I can't believe Nana kept all this. If I could see her and tell her what this means to me…"

"Don't forget her promise. In the next life you'll throw your arms around each other," Nic reminded her.

Laura sniffed. "She made up for every Christmas with this one."

Nic slipped an arm around her shoulders. "She was a unique woman to do all this for you." He pulled her closer and kissed her hair. Laura almost had a heart attack. "What a treasure she has left you. This artwork is very revealing of your talents. Even as young as you were, you drew with spatial accuracy. I'm impressed."

Nic was sitting too close to her. He had no idea what that kiss had done to her. His virility played havoc with her senses. It was impossible to concentrate. "Where's your aunt Susan?"

They looked through the rest of the pictures. He acted as though he hadn't been affected by that impulsive moment, but she could hardly breathe. "I didn't draw any of her. That seems so strange."

"Not really. She wasn't your immediate family. Did she live with you?"

"Oh, no."

"Then that explains it." His arm brushed hers as he helped her put everything back in the box. "For Irene to keep these drawings shows what a loving grandmother she was."

Laura got up from the floor, needing to separate herself from Nic before she did something impulsive and unforgivable. So far her guilt held her back, barely, but she was getting in deeper and deeper.

She'd just lost her grandmother. The thought

of loving Nic and then losing him, too, made her positively ill. *He's not yours to love, Laura.* Her family would never understand. This was a nightmare.

Nic stood to his full height. "It must have torn Irene apart to be separated from you."

CHAPTER FIVE

"YOU'RE RIGHT, *MON FILS.*"

They looked around. Maurice had come into the room.

"She never got over it." His mournful voice pained Laura.

She ran across the expanse to hug him. "Merry Christmas, Maurice. I've never known such a Christmas in my whole life. Thank you with all my heart." She kissed him on both cheeks. "Do you mind if I call you *Gran'père,* too?"

He made a strange sound in his throat and started to weep.

"Come and sit down by the fireplace," she urged him. "Your grandson brought food we can enjoy."

Nic walked over to help. "You'll enjoy the Riesling she bought me. We drank part of it last night, but there's still plenty." He took out the bottle and poured wine into goblets before passing them out. "To you, *Gran'père*."

"*Joyeux Noël.*" Laura followed, but she knew Maurice was overcome with emotion. He took a few sips, but he looked older than his eighty-one years right now. Nervous, she asked, "Would you like to lie down for a while?"

"I think that's a good idea," Nic said. He must have noticed how drained Maurice was, too. "Come on. Let's set you up on the couch and prop your head."

He didn't fight them as they walked him over so he could stretch his legs. "I'm all right," he said with a sigh. "I guess I'm missing Irene too much."

"Of course you are." Laura kissed him again.

"Your parents are hoping to see you before the day is out, *mon fils.*"

Nic nodded. "I'll run over to Marie's a little later."

"Dorine's parents have also arrived there. They know you have a guest, but they'd like to see you at some point."

"I'll do it soon."

Feeling excruciating guilt because she was here and had taken up all Nic's time, Laura looked at him. "Why don't you take care of everything you have to do while Maurice and I enjoy this time together? We have all we need right here."

She could sense his reluctance to leave. He was worried about Maurice. Though she never wanted to be apart from Nic, she had to face reality. "I'm going to stay right here with our *gran'père*. Enjoy the rest of the day with your family, Nic. I'm sure they all miss you terribly. I can only imagine how much Dorine's family is grieving, especially today. You go and don't worry about us."

His dark gray eyes thanked her. "I'll hurry."

After he left, she and Maurice talked for a little while until he fell asleep. The dear thing had done too much, and had worn himself out. She took the time to clean up the mess. Then she read another couple of letters that caught at her heart while she ate the delicious food Arlette had prepared.

"Laura?"

He'd awakened. She walked over with a chair and sat by him. "Feeling better after a catnap?"

"Much, but I was afraid you'd gone."

She smiled. "You can't get rid of me. I'm glad we're alone, because I want to read one of Irene's letters to you. I showed it to Nic earlier. She wrote it from Venice on your tenth wedding anniversary."

A shadow crossed over Maurice's face before he nodded in remembrance.

"Maybe you can answer a question for me." Laura pulled it from her pocket and started in. When she'd finished, she stared at him. "Something terrible happened at the time of your marriage, Maurice. It tore both families apart. I know in my heart you have the answer. Whatever it is, I can take hearing about it."

He blinked. "If I told you, it would do damage that couldn't be repaired. That's why I couldn't tell Irene. It would have destroyed her."

"I knew it was something like that," she whispered. "But you don't have much faith in the Holden women. The truth is, my mother's attitude about you and my grandmother destroyed my happiness years ago. Irene knew you held a secret. If you could tell me what it is, it would help me to put this behind me. And I believe it would help you, too. You've carried the burden far too long. We haven't known each other very long, but I already love you to pieces."

Maurice grasped her hands. "I love you, too. Are you absolutely sure you want to hear this? I've never told this to a living soul. If it had been anyone, I would have told Nic. But when he heard it, he would have done something I couldn't allow to happen."

She knew what Maurice meant. Nic had been so fierce when she'd told him the story that had circulated in her family, it didn't bear thinking about. "You've got me to confide in. Don't forget I'm your granddaughter now and I'm begging you."

He sat up a little. His color had improved since his nap, which was a relief. "All right. It started when Fleurette and I visited your grandfather while he was sick. That's when we met your mother and your aunt."

* * *

When Nic pulled up to the summerhouse four hours later, he noticed Maurice's Renault still there. The sun had already set. His in-laws were coping all right and doing as well as could be expected. But there was a grim atmosphere they'd never be able to shake off until there was news of Dorine, whatever it was.

When Dorine's mother got Nic alone, she'd wanted to hear about Irene's granddaughter and had thought it was wonderful that Laura had come to try to make things right now that Irene had passed away. Nic could tell Dorine's disappearance had changed her mother, who was normally more rigid in her thinking. She'd applauded Laura's desire to mend wounds and said she was proud of Nic for aiding in the process.

"You have to hold close the ones you love while you have the chance. We know all about that, don't we, Nicholas?"

Shattered by more guilt after their conversation, he left for the summerhouse.

He found grandfather and granddaughter watching another DVD. He heard chuckling from both of them. Maurice was sitting in a chair and waved to him. As far as he could tell, the older man felt physically better. Nic was relieved to find him recovered. That was Laura's doing. Despite the storms, she spread sunshine like the six-year-old child Irene had described.

"Come on in, *mon fils*. You've missed all the fun."

"Surely it's not over," Nic teased, his gaze flicking to Laura. She hadn't looked at him yet. That told him something of significance had gone on in his absence.

"I'm afraid it is for me," Maurice stated. "Some of our friends will be coming to the château for the *souper*. I promised to be there." He got up from the chair and kissed Laura before heading for the entrance. "We'll see each other tomorrow."

Nic walked him out to his car. "Why don't I drive you?"

"I'm not too far gone to drive back to the château on my own." Nic frowned. "You two go on enjoying yourselves."

Something had changed. He'd felt it when he'd

first laid eyes on Laura. Now Maurice seemed anxious to leave.

Once back inside the house, he walked over to Laura, who was still sitting in the chair. "What happened here?" The distress on her face was evident. "Did you tell him you were willing the summerhouse back to him?"

She looked up at him. "No. I read him the letter sent from Venice. The moment seemed right. I'm sorry I didn't wait for you."

Nic found a chair. "Did he take it hard?"

"No. I think he was relieved to be able to talk about it. Nic—he's broken the long silence. I now have the missing piece."

He leaned forward, his eyes imploring her. "What did he tell you?"

She moistened her lips nervously. "That my aunt Susan made a play for him when he went to see Irene after they both were free."

"A play, as in—"

"Yes," she answered, reading his mind. "It was something so shocking, I can understand why Maurice never spoke of it."

"What exactly did she do?"

"Let me give you the background first. Susan is eight years older than Mother and was an only child for a long time. I guess when Mother came along, she grew very jealous of her, especially when she married my father. Growing up I saw that jealousy in a lot of ways. Maybe that's why I never drew her in my pictures."

"Jealousy between siblings happens in a lot of families," Nic murmured.

"I know. It's sad that Susan never married, because she's attractive in her own way. But the tragedy here is that after Maurice saw Irene in New York and flew to California to be with her, Susan thought he'd come to see *her*."

"What?" Nic jumped to his feet. "Where on earth would she get an idea like that?"

Laura lowered her head. "Susan had met him those few times when he and your grandmother Fleurette went to visit Richard during his illness. I guess when he came to California again a few years later, Susan was under the impression he'd come to seek her out."

His gray eyes glittered. "She was delusional."

"I agree. But even being older, you know how

charming your grandfather is. In his effort to win my mom and aunt around to the idea of him marrying their mother, he swept Susan off her feet without realizing it. Maurice had no idea and was clueless about her feelings until he returned to the hotel one night and found her waiting for him."

"Laura..."

Unable to sit still, she got to her feet. "By then Susan was thirty-nine and desperate to be married, especially to a handsome, wealthy widower like Maurice Valfort. Possibly she wanted to believe the myth that every Frenchman had a mistress. It's evident the twenty-year age difference didn't matter to her. He's very attractive and looks younger than he is—probably the way you'll look when you get older."

Despite the compliment, Nic shook his head.

"Needless to say, he told her he loved Irene. Susan swung at him in a jealous rage and scratched the side of his jaw. I saw the scar earlier while he was resting."

"That was how he got it?"

"Horrible, isn't it. Susan ran to my mom with

lies that Maurice had not only tried to seduce her, but that he'd seduced their mother while their father was dying."

"Impossible. Fleurette was with him."

"Apparently there was one afternoon when Fleurette didn't go with Maurice because her arthritis had acted up. Susan painted him and Irene as evil people. Because Mother was the younger sister and intimidated by Susan, Mom believed her. Together they told my grandmother that they hated her and Maurice. They said they never wanted to see either of them again in this life. It was exactly as you told me."

"Maurice's only sin was in not telling Irene immediately," Nic broke in. "But he knew how much she adored her daughters and was afraid it would damage Irene forever."

Laura nodded. "You want to know something? I'm glad Irene never knew the truth. It was too ugly."

"Agreed," he emoted.

"To her they were her darling daughters, whatever their faults. Think what your grandfather has been living with all these years…but there's more, Nic."

"What do you mean, more? How could there be?" His eyes were haunted.

"When the two of them married, Susan sent a letter to your great-uncle Auguste, telling him about Maurice's affair with Irene while he and Fleurette went to visit Richard during his illness. Her poison did its damage. *That's* why your family never accepted Irene. In Auguste's words, Maurice had defiled the memory of Fleurette and they didn't consider Irene a God-fearing woman."

Sickness filled Nic's gut.

"Maurice demanded to see the letter. He still has it in his possession."

Nic raked his hands through his hair. "That tale is so horrendous, you couldn't make it up."

"It explains everything. I assured Maurice he'd done the right thing to keep quiet. He broke down and we both cried for a long time. It was cathartic."

"I can imagine." Nic drew closer and put his hands on her shoulders. "You've removed a huge weight from him, but now you're the one I'm worried about."

She managed to put space between them, denying him that moment of closeness. "You don't need to be. I'm so thankful to know the truth. I'm now free to act. Maurice's hands were tied, but mine aren't! I have a phone call to make and I don't care if it's the middle of the night in San Francisco."

"You're sure about this?"

Her jaw hardened the way it had when he'd first met her at Holden headquarters. "I've never been more sure of anything in my life." Laura looked for her purse and pulled out her cell phone.

"Do you want me to leave?"

"No." Her blue eyes beseeched him. "I'm putting this on speakerphone and want you to stay right here. I—I need your support." Her voice faltered. "No more secrets. No more lies."

He agreed. "I'm not going anywhere."

"Thank you." She pressed the digits and soon she heard her mother's voice.

"Laura?" Her mother sounded alarmed. "What's wrong, darling?"

"I'm all right, Mom. I know it's not the best time to be calling, but this couldn't wait."

"Are you still angry with me? Is that what this is about?"

She gripped the phone tighter. "No."

"I'm sorry we quarreled."

"So am I. Please listen to me. I'm calling because you need to come to Nice on the company jet as soon as you can get here. Throw a few things in a suitcase. Your passport is still good."

"Surely you don't mean it."

"But I do, Mom. It's desperately important. I'll tell you everything when you get here. You have to come alone. No Aunt Susan. Do you understand? I need my mother and no one else! Are you at her house?"

"No. I came home earlier this evening. Laura—"

"That's good," she cut her off. "On the way to the airport you can text her that you had to go out of town unexpectedly. No plans you have could be as important as this. I'm begging you to come, Mom. When I meet the plane, I'll answer all your questions."

Laura clicked off so her mother wouldn't keep talking, then she raised her eyes to Nic. "I'm going to force her to face Maurice so she hears the whole truth from him. We'll do it here. He has the letter Susan wrote Auguste and can show it to her. When she knows everything, *you* are going to call the entire Valfort family together and we'll all meet here. Maurice and Irene have been vilified long enough. It's time everyone knew the truth."

"What about your aunt Susan?"

"I'll worry about her later." She smoothed the hair off her forehead. "Do you mind if we go home now and take the box of letters with us? I plan to read all of the ones Irene wrote to Mom and Susan before Mother arrives. I want everything out in the open."

"We'll read them together even if it takes us all night."

Laura lifted moist eyes to him. "I don't know what I'd do without you."

Nic had been thinking the same thing about

her as they loaded up his car and drove back to the villa. Arlette served them a meal in his den while they got comfortable on the couch and started in.

But at two in the morning, he could see and hear her fatigue. "Laura, you need to go to bed. We'll finish these tomorrow after breakfast."

She flashed him a tired smile. "So far there's nothing in these letters but Irene's love. My grandmother truly had no idea about Susan. If she were still alive and could be told the truth, she would probably remember troubling things about her firstborn daughter. But it's clear Irene wasn't a suspicious person."

He got up from the couch. "She was wholesome and wonderful. That's why your grandfather and Maurice couldn't help but be in love with her. You've heard of people everyone loves. Irene was one of them. You may not have been allowed to enjoy her all these years, but I daresay you know her better through these letters and videos than you might have otherwise."

She wiped her eyes. "I think you're right. I

just wish I'd seen her at the end and had been able to wrap my arms around her."

Nic's heart ached for her, but he didn't dare comfort her the way he wanted to. He'd come close to kissing the daylights out of her at the summerhouse. That couldn't happen again. Instead he extended his hand and pulled her to her feet. "Come on. It's time for sleep."

Her eyes had gone a smoky blue. "You're one of the wonderful ones, too. I'm convinced Maurice couldn't have made it all these years without you. You've been his rock even though your world has been torn apart. I admire you immensely, Nic. Thank you for being here for me." She kissed his cheek before leaving the den ahead of him.

When they reached the living room, she turned to him. "Your wife couldn't possibly have gone off with another man, not when she had you for her husband. No matter the truth about her disappearance, be comforted by that thought at least."

Those words gave Nic comfort, but the touch of her lips sent a tremor through him that kept him awake for most of the night. He eventually did sleep, haunted by dreams of her. Dorine wasn't in them. This woman had come out of nowhere to change his world. It would never be the same again.

Nic rose early the next day despite his lack of sleep. Grabbing a cup of coffee from the kitchen, he learned from Arlette that Laura was already up. He walked through the house and discovered she'd gone outside to the garden. This morning she'd dressed in a dusky-blue top and beige pants. He called to her from the terrace. When she turned around, her long blond hair swung onto one shoulder. "Hi!"

He smiled. "How long have you been out here?"

"Just a few minutes."

"Have you heard from your mother yet?"

She sheltered her eyes from a strong sun. "Yes. She'll be in at five this evening."

Pleased with that news for his grandfather's sake, he said, "That means we have plenty of time to do whatever we want. Would you like to go out in the cabin cruiser? It'll be somewhat cool, but it will give you a chance to see Nice from the water. If you get uncomfortable, there's always the afghan."

Her soft laughter warmed him. "I live in San Francisco, remember? I'm used to cooler temperatures than you."

"Then come on up and grab a bite of breakfast with me before we leave."

She left the garden and walked up the stairs toward him. With every step she took, his heart pounded harder.

"Have you had a chance to get in touch with Adam?"

"I let him know I won't be home for a while, but I don't want to talk about him."

Nic had no right to feel the relief that swept through him.

"What about your grandfather?"

"I've told him we plan to meet him at the summerhouse this evening and will be bringing Jessica with us, so he's prepared. Now that you've given me a time, I'll let him know so he can tell the château staff to have dinner ready for us at six."

"That's perfect. Once we've eaten, I'll ask Maurice to tell Mother everything he told me and we'll go from there. I'm going to take the last video she made back to the house so Mom can watch it."

"It might be too much for her," Nic mused aloud. Irene's final words to her family were gut-wrenching.

"Maybe, but she needs to hear and see how much Irene loved her."

"Laura, plan for her to stay in the other bedroom next to yours while she's here." It was the room he'd hoped that one day would be turned into a nursery. Having her mother there would be the buffer he needed to stay away from Laura.

"Thank you. It seems that's all I ever say to you. The debt just keeps growing."

"You're the instrument to bring your mother to France. Maurice owes his future happiness to you. Needless to say, I couldn't be more relieved that this chapter in our lives is going to put an end to the pain for all of us."

"It *has* to." Her voice throbbed. "I'll give her the letters when she goes to bed so she can start reading them. By the time she and I are back home, we'll decide on the best way to handle Susan."

Home to her meant San Francisco. He couldn't think about that right now.

Before long they'd eaten and driven down to the port where he kept his cruiser. He pulled into the private parking area. In a minute he helped her step in the boat and handed her a life jacket. He would have liked to help her on with it, but she thanked him and did it herself, denying him the pleasure of touching her. His desire for her was growing. It terrified him.

"Do you come out in this often?" The breeze blew her hair into enticing disarray.

"When I have the time I bring Maurice fishing with me, or my friends Yves or Luc." He started the motor and headed out at a wakeless speed.

Laura looked all around. "It's the perfect size. What do you catch?"

"Bass and swordfish. Even an occasional tuna."

"I've sailed quite a bit, but I've never been deep-sea fishing."

"You'd love it, unless you have a problem with the *mal de mer*."

"Knowing me, I probably would get seasick in rough seas, but I'd love to try it one day. Did Dorine go out fishing with you?"

"No. Her pursuits were more academic."

"To each his or her own poison, right?"

He grinned. She had a great attitude about life. "All you have to do is ask if you want to go fishing while you're here, but since we can't be out all day, let's forgo that pleasure today and I'll give you a tour of the sights closer to shore."

"Perfect!"

They took off and cruised for a time without saying anything.

Those heavenly blue eyes scanned the coastline. "It may be winter, but Nice has a subtropical appearance, with all the palm and citrus fruit trees."

"That's why people from around the world come here to vacation in winter. For your information, we're in one of the large bays, called Villefrance-sur-mer, which is enclosed. In a minute we'll pass the main expanse of Nice, between the old port city and the airport, by crossing another bay."

She studied the terrain. "What mountains are those?"

"The western edge of the Ligurian Alps."

"Irene and Maurice must have explored a lot of this." Her gaze suddenly swung to his. "They *were* happy, weren't they? Despite their pain?"

Her anguished cry had surfaced. All the time they'd been making small talk, he'd been waiting for it to emerge. She was seated across from him. He cut the motor. "Come here, Laura."

She almost stumbled into his arms getting there. Nic pulled her onto his lap. Despite her life jacket, he crushed her against him. For a little while he held her tight while the breeze rocked the cruiser.

When she finally raised her head, her cheeks were wet. "I'm sorry to break down like this."

"Hush," he whispered, kissing each feature the way he'd done in his dreams. Once he found her lips, his mouth closed over hers, needing her the way he needed air to breathe. Her mouth trembled, driving him to seek deeper until she opened up to him. He heard her small groan of pleasure as fire leaped between them.

Nic couldn't fight his desire for her another second. He would never stop loving Dorine, but Laura was right here with him, giving him one kiss, then another. The giving and taking went on and on. Each one grew longer and more passionate. He felt himself drowning in ecstasy. To be loving again like this after so long—he couldn't believe it.

She filled his arms, his heart. Who would have thought Irene's death would have resulted in this wonderful woman coming into his life? If she could respond to him like this, then whatever she felt for Adam was too pale in comparison to matter.

"Do you have any idea how much I want you?"

he whispered against her throat. "I've never felt like this in my life. I feel so guilty. Believe me when I tell you I've been trying to honor Dorine's memory."

"So have I," she murmured in an aching voice. "You must think me so terrible. I need to go home."

"Laura, there's no way I'm going to let you leave me. I need you, and I *know* you need me."

He embraced her with refined savagery. Besides her beauty he loved her sweetness, her strength and intelligence. Her fun-loving ways. She was so natural and real. "Talk to me, *mon amour*. Tell me what I want to hear," he cried. But when he started to devour her again, she wrenched her lips from his.

"I—I can't say the words you want to hear, Nic. We can't do this!"

"We already have" came the fierce response before he sought her mouth again with a consuming hunger neither of them could deny or satisfy. Once he'd met and married Dorine, he'd never wanted another woman. After she'd gone missing, he hadn't been able to imagine wanting any woman, not ever again. But he hadn't met Irene's granddaughter...

"This isn't right." She half moaned the words when he let her up for air.

He closed his eyes tightly. "Because you're committed to Adam?" Nic didn't want to think about her return to the States. "You couldn't be madly in love with him or you could never kiss me like this." His eyes blazed into hers. "Have you ever kissed him with the kind of urgency and passion you've just shown me?"

She buried her face in his shoulder.

That had to be his answer, but he needed to hear the words. "Answer me, Laura." Was her bond with Adam stronger than Nic wanted to believe?

"Adam's not the reason this has to end. You're a married man, Nic. While there's still a wedding ring on your finger, no matter how much I might desire you, this is wrong—"

"Laura—"

"Don't say any more." She sounded frantic. "You're still looking for your wife." She grabbed the lapels of his Windbreaker. "I want you to find her. Even after three years, she could still be alive somewhere, waiting for help, waiting to get back to the man she loves."

He caressed the side of her neck with his hand, kissing her with growing hunger. "For the first year I believed she was alive. But two years have passed since then." His voice grated. "I sense she's gone."

"Even so, there has to be a part of your heart that hasn't given up yet. I know it hasn't and I won't give up on her either."

Laura moved off his lap and returned to the seat opposite him. "You and I have been caught up in two family tragedies we're still sorting out. My emotions are ragged and so are yours. Naturally I'm not going to forget what happened between us just now. We're both human and turned to each other for comfort. But let's put it behind us, where it has to stay."

He raked a hand through his hair. Though he felt Dorine was dead, he didn't have absolute proof. In that sense Laura was right—this was still a betrayal of his wife if there was the slight-est chance she was alive. Nic had never been so

conflicted in his life. Because of the precarious-
ness of their situation right now, he was willing to go along with Laura, but only to a point.

"Let's get back to the car." Once he'd started
kissing her, he'd lost track of time. He started
the motor and they once again shot through
the water toward the port. "With all the traffic,
we'll be lucky to pick up your mother on time."

Even though they weren't touching, he could
feel how shaken she was. After they reached
the car, she opened her purse and started to
brush her hair. Then came the lipstick. By the
time they reached the airport a half hour later,
she'd restored herself. But Nic still discerned
the heightened color that revealed what they'd
been doing out on the water.

A few minutes later Jessica Tate emerged
from the Holden corporate jet. The moment
Nic saw her, he understood Laura's earlier
comment about no one thinking she and her
mother looked alike. She had brown hair and
was shorter, yet attractive in her own way, especially for a woman in her mid-fifties.

She wore a good-looking two-piece suit in a

melon color and a single strand of pearls. All three Holden women had exceptional dress sense. Though he picked out certain similar familial characteristics, it was a different experience than his first glimpse of Laura, whose resemblance to Irene had left him staggered.

Laura hugged her mother and spoke privately with her for a few minutes. Then she put an arm around her waist and walked her over to Nic.

"Mom? This is Nicholas Valfort, Maurice's grandson. Nic, please meet my mother, Jessica Tate, Irene and Richard's second daughter."

CHAPTER SIX

"Jessica. I've been anxious to meet you."

The blue eyes were like Laura's in color, but they stared at him without warmth. "How do you do, Mr. Valfort." She turned to her daughter. "Will you please tell me what's going on? I'm very uncomfortable. You made it sound like this was a life-and-death situation."

"It is, Mom. My life and Maurice's."

Nic eyed Laura. A nerve was hammering at the base of her throat, revealing her tension. "Excuse me while I put her suitcase in the car."

"Where are we going?" Jessica demanded after Laura climbed in the backseat with her. Nic was already at the wheel and watched them in the rearview mirror. Only a little while ago she'd been in his arms and they'd kissed each other with an abandon he hadn't thought possible. He'd never be able to put it from his mind.

"If you recall, Irene left me something in her will. It's a house on the Valfort estate, the one Maurice lived in with her. We're going there now to have dinner."

Her mother's face filled with alarm. "I can't."

"Yes, you can. You *have* to!"

As he drove them to the château, Nic marveled at Laura's courage to deal with this tragedy head-on.

"Did you receive the money Nana left you and Susan? Maurice had the attorney send it to Holden headquarters."

Jessica looked at a complete loss. "I haven't seen any money."

"Then check with Aunt Susan," said Laura. "I'm sure she has taken charge of it."

"Why do you say that?"

Her bewilderment convinced Nic that Laura's mother wasn't the architect of the horror story that had torn families apart.

"Because she has run your life ever since I can remember. In the process, she ruined all our lives. Your sister is a sick, manipulative woman. Because of her lies, she not only deprived us of your mother and my grandmother, she poisoned Maurice's family against him and Irene."

"How can you say that?" her mother cried.

"Because it's true. In a few minutes we're meeting with Maurice."

Jessica shook her head. "No. Don't try to force me."

"Mom, you owe this to him and to us. Our three lives are on the line. Susan ruined the Valforts' happiness and ours. I need you here so together we can make amends to Maurice and his loved ones before we fly back to San Francisco. He'll tell you just how disturbed Susan was and still is. You're not going to like it, but when you've heard everything, you'll understand that she needs psychiatric help. However, we'll talk about that later. Right now it's not too late to rectify the situation with his family."

Nic grimaced. Touched as he was by Laura's desire to make certain the Valfort family knew the whole truth, the thought of her leaving Nice was unacceptable to him.

When he drove up in front of the summerhouse, Maurice opened the doors and walked out to greet Jessica. "It's been a long time since I last saw you. Your mother and I waited many years to see you cross over this threshold. Thank you for coming."

Laura turned to her mother, who looked frightened, before she said something that surprised Nic. "Mom? You and Maurice need to spend this evening alone. Here's a DVD Nana made for you and me. At the right time, Maurice will show it to you." Laura's eyes darted to Nic, imploring him to go along with this, before she eyed her mother again. "When you're ready, we'll come back for you. Tonight you'll be staying with me at Nic's villa."

Maurice gave Laura a kiss on the cheek.

"I hope I did the right thing." Laura's voice shook after Nic helped her back in the car. The other two had gone inside the house.

"Was there any doubt? I know my grandfather inside and out. That kiss was his way of letting you know he was grateful for the time alone with your mother." He started the engine and drove away.

"This has to work, Nic."

He reached out to squeeze her arm before releasing it. "It will, but it'll be a long night for them. I suggest we drive into Nice and have our own dinner at a café bar I think you'll enjoy. The seafood menu is traditional Nicoise— snails, clams, blue oysters, shrimp. Take your pick. But if you're a pasta lover, we can—"

"I prefer fish whenever possible. You've sold me. Can we do takeout?"

"Bien sûr."

"Then why don't we get some and drive to the technology park? I'd like to see where you work."

Laura didn't dare to go a place to eat where there might be dancing. She couldn't handle being in his arms one more time. They'd crossed a line. He'd loved Dorine enough to marry her and was still a married man.

She was tortured by it and vowed never to get that close to him again. But she could satisfy her longing to get to know him better by learning more about where he worked, what made him tick.

He drove to the Place Garibaldi, where she

waited for him to get their food. Once back in the car with a bag, he headed for the main route leading away from the city center. "My work is about ten minutes from here."

"How nice for you."

"It's definitely convenient."

Pretty soon they came to a turnoff. "What does that sign say?"

"We're entering Sophia Antipolis. It's regarded as one of the world's most prestigiouscenters for voluntary integrated economic development."

"There you go again, speaking over my head."

He chuckled. "It's called a technopole. There are twelve hundred companies with seventy countries represented here."

"How incredible!" They drove deeper into the park with its heavy foliage. "Oh look, Rue Albert Einstein. When you think of the French Riviera, somehow you don't associate a humongous brain trust with brilliant minds like yours all working together here."

"Some more brilliant than others," he quipped. "It has pine-covered hills, hiking trails, jogging paths, a riding stable, golf courses and reflecting pools." They wound around until he pulled in a parking space near one of the buildings: Valfort Technologies.

"You don't need to take me inside, Nic. I just wanted to see it. You work in a world all its own."

"That was the original idea." He turned off the engine and handed her a carton with a fork. They began eating.

"Um." She tested the clams first. "This seafood is excellent."

"I'm glad you like it."

"Did your wife work close by?" Where Nic was concerned, her curiosity was insatiable.

"About five minutes from here by car."

"Did you meet jogging or horseback riding?"

"Neither. She wasn't that great a driver and failed to stop at one of the intersections. She hit the rear end of my car."

"Uh-oh. But when you got out to inspect the damage, you immediately forgave her when you saw how adorable she was."

One side of his mouth lifted in a smile. "You're right."

"Was she your first love?"

"No. I had several relationships over the years before our accident."

"What happened that you didn't end up with one of them?"

"Though my parents are happy enough, I wanted a marriage like Maurice and Irene's. Somehow the reality never lived up to the spiritual essence I was hoping for."

"Until you met Dorine."

"Ours was more a meeting of the minds."

This trip to Nice had taught Laura one invaluable truth. She knew that when she went back to San Francisco, she was going to end it with Adam. Theirs was not that one heart, one soul mating, the kind Nic had just referred to when he'd talked about their grandparents.

"I'm surprised you aren't married yet," Nic murmured. "That means you've turned down a lot of men already."

Her brows lifted. "You think?"

"I know." His husky tone sent shivers down her spine.

"By high school I had my sights set on the

corporate office. Mother told me that if I wanted to make it in business, I shouldn't let romance distract me. She told me I had years before I needed to worry about marriage. When I started working there and saw the number of fouled-up office relationships, I made up my mind to put business first."

His eyes gleamed in the semidarkness. "How long have you known Adam?"

She sighed. "He was moved into the accounting office from San Jose about a year ago. We were introduced and—"

"That was it for him," Nic broke in. "Is that when you amended your decision not to get involved?"

"No. I didn't start dating him until October. On Thanksgiving he took me to meet his parents. Adam comes from a fine family. His parents are so stable."

"But what about your feelings for him?"

She averted her eyes.

"I shouldn't have asked that question, but you remind me of myself when I was trying to decide whether to marry Dorine or not. I enjoyed her family very much. And family—or the lack of it—is of vital importance, as we both know."

"You're right."

"So tell me, what are the qualities that attract you to Adam?"

The questions were painful because Nic was getting closer and closer to the truth about her feelings for Adam. "He's attractive and clever. I can tell he's ambitious, but that isn't necessarily a bad thing for business."

"Maurice would agree with you. To make a company succeed, you have to have fire in the belly, but sometimes that quality is hard on personal relationships."

Laura nodded. "My mother feels he's a little too eager beaver."

"You're a Holden," he blurted. "She's entitled to want to protect her only chick from the fortune hunters out there."

She stopped eating. "You saw right through that, didn't you."

"Don't forget I'm a Valfort. Fortune hunters come male and female."

"Yet you knew that wasn't the case with Dorine."

"My wife was raised with the good things in life and had more than money on her mind."

Laura smiled at him. "You're talking about her brain, the kind that understands what *you're* talking about. You two had your own private club. How wonderful." She closed the carton she'd emptied, envious for that kind of loving relationship. "I'm so sorry for what happened to you I can hardly fathom it."

"Though I didn't think it possible at the beginning, I'm doing better these days. Your coming to Nice has helped in remarkable ways. No one in my family will talk about Dorine. They're afraid of hurting me, and that's understandable. But it's felt good to open up to you."

"I'm glad. One of my friends married a soldier who returned from Iraq with PTSD. They're the ones who have the little boy I spoke about. Through counseling she learned that he needed to talk about his experiences. It helped him a lot once he could share the pain with her, no matter how hideous or traumatizing. Not talking about it is the worst thing you can do.

"The counselor explained that PTSD doesn't just happen to soldiers. You've gone through a life-altering experience, Nic, and need to talk about it and your life with her. How are her parents holding up?"

"They're strong, and they have each other. It's the waiting for news of any kind that's been hard on them."

"Of course. Do you talk to them every day?"

"Not as much during this last year. Their lives are busy."

"I'm sure you're a great comfort to them. I know you have close family, but I assume you and Maurice have relied on each other the most for emotional support."

He put his empty carton back in the sack. "Always. Let's hope he and your mother are going to find relief before the night is over."

She rested her head against the window. "I wonder how it's really going with them."

"So far no phone call."

"I know. It has to be a good sign, doesn't it?"

His gaze wandered over her. When he looked at her like that, she found it hard to breathe. "You're anxious. Do you want to go back home?"

No. But much as she wished they could stay right here and keep on talking, she knew it was for the best that they leave. What had happened on his cruiser could easily happen again if she gave in to her longing for him. "Maybe we ought to, just in case."

She had the impression he didn't want to go anywhere, either, but after hesitating he started the engine. Nic was riddled with guilt. She could feel it, and she loved him for his devotion to his wife. Their situation was impossible. "By the time we get there, your mother might call you. Fortunately the villa's not that far from the estate."

The villa was his home. *And Dorine's.* But there was a problem, because Laura had started thinking of it as home, too. When she imagined returning to her condo in San Francisco, the realization that Nic wouldn't be there filled her with an emptiness that refused to go away.

While they drove back, she couldn't help staring at his compelling profile. "I meant what I said the other day. I'm going to give the summerhouse back to Maurice. He needs his own place. I believe it will be a great comfort for him to continue living where he knew such happiness with Irene. As long as he has his health, he needs his independence. You know very well he doesn't want to live with your father and mother. Not yet, anyway."

He glanced at her. "I would ask you how you got so smart, but then I remember you're Irene's granddaughter."

"In the morning, will you go with me to get the legal work done?"

"Since I can see your mind is made up, I guess I don't have a choice."

She smiled. "Good. With that fait accompli, Maurice will be able to get on with his life. He can continue overseeing the Valfort empire from the summerhouse. Set him up with a computer that's linked to the mainframe. Depending on the longevity of the Valfort genes, he could conceivably be running the company for years yet."

"Better watch out," he murmured. "He might decide to steal you from Holden headquarters and give you a prominent position as his executive assistant."

Don't hold out that idea to me, Nic. We can't think that way. We can't have a future.

"He'd never do that to your family. It would start another war."

Lines marred his handsome features at the thought. Little did he know her body quickened at the very suggestion she work for his grandfather. To live here in Nice and be so close to him... But it was impossible.

"I'll be perfectly happy to remain his American granddaughter."

"Neither of you will feel that way if you're on the other side of the Atlantic, out of reach."

She wished he hadn't said that. Didn't he realize there was no hope?

While she was waiting for her mother's call, Nic's cell phone rang. After he answered, the conversation went on for a few minutes. She'd been nervous enough, but now she feared the meeting between her mother and Maurice hadn't gone well. Her body tensed in apprehension.

"What's wrong?" she asked the moment he hung up.

"Are you prepared to learn that a miracle has happened? Maurice showed her the DVD before they began talking. Your mother was so over-come by it, she asked him to tell her the truth of everything the moment it ended. It was quite a conversation. After he showed her the letter Susan had sent to Auguste, she broke down and begged his forgiveness. Their meeting couldn't have gone better."

"Thank heaven." It was Laura's turn to fall apart with relief.

"Your mother asked if she could talk to his family. He made a call and then drove her to the château, where she met with my parents and Auguste."

Hot tears trickled down her cheeks. "I—I can't believe it."

"They've all been talking, and now she wants us to come and get her."

She sniffed. "I'm surprised Mom can even function."

"I don't think I am," he said on a solemn note. "You have Irene's strength. It seems that having heard the truth, your mother does, too. This has made a new man of my grandfather. I could hear it in his voice."

The next hour turned out to be a revelation. After they arrived at the château, Maurice introduced Laura to the assembled group. At last she met Nic's family, who seemed genuinely sorrowful for the part they'd played in judging Irene.

His parents were very gracious to Laura. They commented on her strong likeness to Irene. Interestingly enough, Nic only faintly resembled his mother and father. He was Maurice's grandson in every way.

As the night wore on, one glance at her mother and she could tell Jessica was almost ready to faint from all the strain. Nic saw it too and suggested it was time to leave.

Maurice walked them out to the car. He gave Laura a tender hug while Nic helped her mother into the backseat. Finally Laura climbed in next to her. "Talk to you tomorrow, *Gran'père,*" she called out.

All was quiet after they started down the drive, but Laura's heart thudded with anxiety.

"Mom?"

"I'm all right, darling." She grasped Laura's hand. "The question is, how do you feel, and can you ever forgive me?"

"Now that we know the truth, there's nothing to forgive. We owe Maurice everything because he never told Nana about Susan. I'm glad I didn't know about it until now, and I love him for sparing all of us that horror."

"Mother was right. He's a wonderful man. She said that when we all meet in heaven one day, we'll throw our arms around each other and all will be forgiven."

"Oh, Mom." Laura hugged her for a long time.

"I've already forgiven Susan and know you have, too. She's not in her right mind. Susan was always different, but I never suspected her problems went so deep. I don't think the videos or the letters would be helpful to her in her condition."

Laura kissed her mom's cheek. "I agree."

"Tomorrow I'm flying back to San Francisco and will talk to a psychiatrist about the best way to handle her. Are you coming with me?"

She couldn't leave Nic yet. Not yet… "I can't. Tomorrow I'm going to see an attorney and have papers drawn up to give the summerhouse back to Maurice."

Jessica didn't fight her on it. "Your nana knew what she was doing when she left it to you."

"I'm sure she hoped this would be the outcome. When I've packed the things she gave me, I'll fly home."

"How soon do you have to be back at work?"

"Not until after New Year's."

Her mother squeezed her hand harder. "Because of Susan, I judged Maurice and Mother, and will always be sorry for keeping you from her. But it's not too late for me to ask your forgiveness for judging Adam. He's in love with you. Forget what I said about him. If you love him, then so do I. That's all that matters."

On a burst of deep emotion, Laura held on to her mother until they reached the house without saying anything. It was over with Adam.

The only man she loved was Nic. She couldn't imagine a future without him, but she would have to deal with that reality, because he was still married. If by some miracle his wife were returned to him unharmed, it still wouldn't change her feelings for him. Unless another man came along who could make her forget Nic Valfort, she was doomed to go through life alone.

Jessica's sentiments to Laura drifted forward to torment Nic. The only thing that saved him was the knowledge that Laura wasn't going home tomorrow. Hopefully the legal matter would take several days to resolve, delaying her departure for as long as possible.

He drove them back to the villa. While Laura got her mother settled in the other guest bedroom, he went to the den to check his voice mail. No call from the detective yet. His assistant, Robert, had called to ask for a few more days off because extended family was still visiting. Nic phoned and told him to take all the time he wanted. Right now he intended to spend every second possible with Laura.

There was a second call from Yves, his good friend from childhood who'd gone through a nasty divorce two years ago and was still trying to recover. He suggested they get together over drinks before the holidays were over. Yves had helped in the search for Dorine. Nic owed him and still had a Christmas gift for him.

Why not set things up for tomorrow night? He'd invite Laura to go with him. It would be a legitimate way to take her out for an evening. Yves would probably bring a girlfriend. His friend wouldn't think anything about Laura being with Nic when he learned she was Irene's granddaughter. In fact he'd see the resemblance, since he'd been at the summerhouse with Nic many times over the years, before and after Nic's marriage.

Once he'd made the phone call, he walked back to the living room, where he found Laura waiting for him.

"I wanted to touch base with you before I go

to bed. Mother has made arrangements with the pilot to fly out tomorrow morning at nine. She'll phone for a taxi. I just wanted you to know I'll go with her to see her off."

He frowned. "Would she rather I didn't drive her?"

Color rushed into her cheeks. "No—" She put her hands out. "It's nothing like that. She doesn't want to intrude on your hospitality any more than necessary."

"It's no intrusion. She's Irene's daughter and your mother."

"I know, but don't forget how terrible she feels deep down. She needs time."

Nic nodded. "In that case, take my car. I have another one in the garage if I need it. To make it easier, I'll make myself scarce in the morning." He pulled out his keys and took the Mercedes key off the ring.

Her blue gaze looked darker than usual before she reached for it. Their fingers brushed. If her emotions were in as much turmoil as his, then she was barely holding on. "You belong to a family with a forgiving nature. They couldn't have been kinder to Mother or me. Now I know why you're a prince."

"Laura—" His voice came out sounding husky to his own ears.

"It's true." Her eyes clung to his. "A miracle happened to the Valfort and Holden families tonight, but I'm greedy because I'm praying for another one. The one that brings your lovely wife safely home to you. I mean that with all my heart. Good night."

He stood there long after she'd gone to bed, trying to get a grip on his feelings. Nic had no doubt she meant what she said. It might have only been a few days, but he'd learned enough about Laura's character to know she would never entertain an affair with him. Whatever physical and emotional bond they'd forged out on the boat, she wouldn't act on it, because she wasn't that kind of woman.

He wasn't that kind of man.

If Dorine were never found, it would be four more years before she would be declared legally dead. Four more years before he could even *think* about getting married again to any woman, *if* that's what he desired.

But after four years Laura wouldn't be available, let alone still wanting to be with him.

No matter how he looked at it, a relationship with her was out of the question. Deep down in his gut, he realized she'd just sent him a coded message. Without saying the exact words, she'd told him that she intended to go home soon. And whether or not she married Adam, she'd keep her distance from Nic.

He turned out the lights and headed for his bedroom, knowing sleep might not come to him tonight.

After taking her mother to the airport the next morning, Laura returned to the villa. She found Nic at his desk in the den on the phone. Realizing he was busy, she started to walk out, but he motioned for her to stay where she was. His all-encompassing glance sent her pulse off the charts.

"How was your mother this morning?" he asked after hanging up the phone.

"Anxious to get back and meet with a doctor who knows how to treat a situation like this. Mom has needed therapy for years. Now she'll get it."

"What about you? How are you holding up?"

"Now that there are no secrets, I'm doing better than I would have thought. You're the one I'm worried about."

He shook his dark head. "You don't need to be. From here on out things are going to be different in my family. Vastly improved." One black brow lifted. "That's a relief only *you* could understand."

"A weight has been taken from both our shoulders, but you sustain a pain that doesn't leave you alone."

"I've been living with it for three years. And don't forget I have my work, which is flourishing."

"I don't doubt it." She sighed. "Speaking of work, I'm facing mounds of it when I get back. I've implemented some new marketing incentives at a few hotels around the state and need to follow the results closely. It means I'll be traveling for a while."

His features sobered. "Sounds like you're anxious to get back. To expedite things, I've retained an attorney for you," he announced, "but he won't be available until tomorrow. Unless you have other plans, I've arranged for a moving company to meet us at the summerhouse at noon with some boxes. We'll get everything packed up and they'll store them. When you're ready to fly home, they'll load them on the company jet."

"A man who can move mountains. That's you."

He got to his feet and moved closer to her. A tightness around his eyes and mouth revealed his suffering. "Would that I could divine where to look for Dorine."

Laura would give anything to help him. He needed an ending. "Nic—after all this time, what do your instincts tell you?"

She waited a good minute for his answer. "Unless I was married to a woman who was unbalanced or kept secrets and was operating with an unknown agenda—destructive or otherwise—my feeling is that she was kidnapped. That's the detective's hunch, too."

"I think you're probably right."

"What happened to her after that I've tried not to think about."

Laura shuddered. "Was her purse missing?"

"Yes, along with her cell phone. It has never been used, or a credit card. No emails, no bank account accessed. Nothing. Our combined families have offered an enormous reward for her safe return, but it never happened."

"Maybe she was at the wrong place at the wrong time. If she went out during her lunch hour, maybe food wasn't on her mind and she decided to do a little shopping or run an errand."

"All the secretary said was that Dorine was leaving for her lunch break."

Laura sighed. "Yes, it's not much to go on."

"No, but I remember her saying Dorine was working on a project that needed to get finished. I assumed that meant she'd intended to hurry."

"What kind of project was it? Would she

have needed to buy something in order to complete it?"

"They have technicians for that."

"Maybe she went out to get some information she needed."

He gave her a resigned smile. "Now you're playing the maybe game. In the beginning I played it until I drove myself mad."

"I can understand that." She'd been pacing the floor but came to a standstill. "The police would have combed that neighborhood where her car was found."

"Thoroughly. So did I on my own time. My hunch was that she must have gone in a store or building where she was abducted away from the street through a rear entrance. It could have been a business where she was a regular and knew them. Or they knew her and watched for her. The car showed no evidence of foul play or a struggle. No fingerprints were picked up except hers."

Laura hunched her shoulders. "Or there's the possibility she was abducted in the technology park with all that heavy foliage. Someone who knew her and her habits could have stopped her on some pretext after she left the office."

He cocked his head. "You're thinking she knew him?"

"Yes. Maybe someone from the team who had an accomplice. While one dealt with her, the other could have driven her car into town and left it there to throw the police off the trail. Nic, did the authorities question the companies within the park?"

"Yes. Every one of them," he said in a grating tone.

"What about the woods? Did they search them?"

His black-fringed eyes darkened until she couldn't see the gray. "Only near her office building."

"Why not the whole park?"

"You're talking six thousand acres."

"I had no idea it was so huge. But if the crime happened in the park, then the whole place should be scoured. If the police used dogs, they might turn up some evidence."

He studied her for a long time. The stretch of

silence told her to stop talking because she'd taken this painful inquisition too far.

"I'm sorry, Nic. Forgive me for getting into this with you when you've tried to put it behind you."

His hands reached out to grip her shoulders. He shook her gently. "There's nothing to forgive. You've only put voice to my own thoughts. The park could be hiding many secrets. I marvel that you've given it this much consideration. It means more to me than you know."

You mean more to me than you know, Nic. "I want to help you the way you've helped me."

A groan escaped his throat before he put her away from him with a reluctance she sensed. It was a good thing he let go of her when he did— another second and she wouldn't have been able to stop herself from kissing him, with or without his permission.

"I told you last night, being able to talk to you about Dorine has been cathartic for me. I'm going to talk to the detective about doing a massive ground search of the entire park and vehicles."

Her spirits lifted. "I know it will take hundreds of men and man-hours and the cost will be prohibitive, but if they can turn up even one clue…"

"Cost be damned! I'll spend any amount to find out what happened to her," he muttered fiercely.

Yes, she mused to herself, because he was a man who loved deeply and was the most exceptional human being she'd ever known. Before she broke down and told him how she felt, she looked at her watch. "I think we'd better leave for the summerhouse or the movers will get there first."

"You're right." But he sounded far away.

They gathered their things and went out to his car. On the drive, he darted her a speculative glance. "If it sounds good to you, we're going to have dinner tonight at the Gros Marin. You can't go back to the States without eating there. Nice's finest restaurant hovers right over the sand and serves delicious Mediterranean seafood. You'll enjoy the sight of the yachts all lit up."

The thought of returning to California was killing her. "It sounds lovely."

"Yves LeVaux, my best friend from childhood, will be joining us."

Though she'd give anything to spend the evening alone with him, the addition of another person would provide the necessary buffer. "Is your friend married?"

"Divorced. He may bring someone with him. We haven't seen each other in a while. Yves helped me during the initial search for Dorine."

"What a wonderful friend," she murmured.

"The best. I'm indebted to him."

Laura's sorrow dragged her down. If Nic's wife were never found, he'd suffer from this tragedy his whole life.

Soon after they reached the summerhouse, the movers arrived and they spent the rest of the day packing. Once the cartons were put on the truck and the men left, Laura helped Nic take down the Christmas tree and decorations and put everything away. He carried the tree outside seemingly effortlessly while she cleaned and vacuumed.

"Now Maurice can move back in," she said when he walked into the room. "After I've been to see the attorney tomorrow, let's bring your grandfather here and tell him what I've done. If he doesn't want to live here again, maybe someone else in the Valfort family will want to take up residence. Possibly one of your cousins? Is anyone in the family planning to get married?"

"Not yet, but it could happen before long. Since our work here is finished, I'll drive us back to the villa to get changed for dinner."

On the way home Laura thought about what to wear. She hadn't planned to be here long and had only brought one dress for evening. It was a black crepe kimono-sleeve wrap dress with a high neck. The hem fell to the knee. She'd been to several marketing dinners in it.

When they reached the house, she disappeared into the bathroom to wash her hair and blow-dry it. Deciding to leave it long, she brushed it before applying lipstick and some blusher. Once she'd put on her dress and had slipped into her sling-back black heels, she walked into the living room and discovered Nic had a guest. He stood by the French doors facing the garden below. It drew everyone's attention.

The good-looking dark blond man in the tan suit was probably six feet. When he heard her come in, he wheeled around and fastened warm hazel eyes on her. "So you're the missing granddaughter, Laura Tate," he said with a strong French accent, and walked over to her.

"Guilty as charged." *And filled with guilt.*

His eyes filled with male appreciation. "Your resemblance to Irene is amazing. I'm Yves LeVaux." They shook hands.

"Nic told me what a great friend you are to him. It's a pleasure to meet you."

"I'll return the compliment. He said to come in and make myself at home while he got ready. I'm glad I did. Since his wife disappeared, you have the distinction of being the only woman to capture his attention, let alone step inside this house. I for one am delighted to see it happen."

She'd known Nic was an honorable man. He couldn't be anything else. Now his friend had just confirmed it. Unfortunately Yves had the wrong idea about them. "As I told his house-keeper, Nic and I are almost family."

He flashed her a curious smile. "But the point is, you're not."

Laura took a quick breath. "The more important point is, he's married."

Yves's smile faded. "So was the man my wife had an affair with. No doubt Nic told you I'm divorced."

She felt his pain. "I'm so sorry, Yves. They were both fools."

His brows lifted. "I think so, too. Anyway, where have you been all day, let alone my life?"

Despite his grief, he could still be charming. It was a trait shared by the three Frenchmen she knew. "We just came back from the summer-house. My grandmother left me a lot of gifts. I was getting them packed to take home."

"But let's hope that won't be for a while. I'd like to get to know you better. How soon do you plan to leave?"

"That's a good question," Nic answered in his deep voice before she could say anything.

With thudding heart, she turned in time to see

him approach with a small Christmas present in his hand. The light gray suit with the charcoal shirt fit Nic's well-honed body to perfection. Laura's mouth went dry just looking at him.

After his slow appraisal that brought heat to her face, his gaze slid from her to his friend. "I see you two have already met." Nic handed Yves the present. "No date tonight?"

Yves shook his head. With a half smile he said, "I decided I wanted to have a good time for a change."

Laura couldn't help but chuckle. "That was honest."

He trained his eyes on her again. "I see honesty is something we have in common. Did Nic tell you I haven't had much luck meeting the right woman?"

She decided she liked him very much. "Finding the right man is a tall order for a woman, too. You're still young and there's plenty of time."

"Your grandmother told me the same thing the last time I saw her."

A lump lodged in her throat. "I'm jealous of

you and Nic. Both of you spent time with her. It's my fault I didn't get to know her, so anything you can tell me about her, I'll relish."

"Have you got a month or two?" Yves teased with a twinkle in his eyes.

"I wish." *If I could have a lifetime here...* "But I have to get back to my job." She needed to get away from Nic before she changed her mind and took up residence in the summerhouse.

"Nic tells me you're the marketing manager for Holden Hotels. That speaks highly of your business acumen. Your grandfather was never one for nepotism." Before she could say anything, he exchanged glances with Nic. "Mind if I open my present before we go?"

"Be my guest, *mon ami*."

Yves undid the wrapping and opened the box. *"épatant!"* He held up a three-inch gold lure.

"It's the latest Shimano waxwing," Nic explained. "In the fall I caught some amazing fish with one just like it. Next time we go out together, you should try it."

"I plan to. *Merci, mon vieux*."

"*De rien.* Do you want to drive with us to the Gros Marin?"

"No. I'll follow you in my car. My folks are expecting me to drop by their house later."

"Then let's go."

CHAPTER SEVEN

Two hours later the three of them left the restaurant and walked over to Yves's car. He hadn't taken his eyes off Laura throughout their dinner. "This was the best time I've had in ages," he said, smiling at Nic.

"My sentiments exactly. We'll get together soon and do some fishing."

Yves nodded before his hazel gaze swerved to Nic's houseguest once more. "You'll really be gone after New Year's?"

"Afraid so. Business calls. Until then I hope to spend as much time as possible with Maurice."

"Lucky man." He winked at her before getting in his car. "*À bientôt,* Nic." His parting comment was an afterthought. Nic could tell Yves had been blown away by Laura.

After his friend drove off, Nic escorted her to

his car. "If you stayed in Nice any longer, Adam would be in for serious competition."

She smoothed some hair behind her ear. "Yves is hurting. I hope he can find someone who appreciates what a terrific man he really is."

He helped her in the car, then went around to get behind the wheel. "That's been my hope for quite some time."

"I'm sure it will happen. When it does, *she'll* be the lucky one."

Nic put his key in the ignition, but he didn't turn the car on. He flashed her a glance, eager to spend the rest of the evening with her doing something that had nothing to do with other people. It was impossible not to feel possessive of her tonight. "The evening's still young. How would you like to see a sight you'll never forget?"

Her smile captivated him. "That's a trick question. After arousing my curiosity, even if I told you I'm too tired, I couldn't possibly say no."

Laura...

"I promise you won't be sorry. It's only twelve kilometers away." He joined one of the arterials headed east. "It's been my experience that America has some of the great road movies, but it's my country that has the great roads. Do you remember that scene in *To Catch a Thief* with Cary Grant and Grace Kelly, when she was driving the sports car?"

"I must have watched that cliff-hanger scene half a dozen times."

"It was filmed on the Grande Corniche, the stunning coastal highway we're traveling on right now. The engineering feat was built to facilitate Napoleon's Italian campaign. We'll drive to the little medieval village at the top called Eze. At fourteen hundred feet above sea level, it perches like an eagle's nest. You can see everything from that vantage point."

They rode in silence, but the tension between them was building by degrees. Once they reached the summit, Laura let out an exclamation. The ancient little town set on a narrow rocky peak overlooked the Mediterranean.

He pointed to a ruin in the distance. "Those are the remains of a twelfth-century castle. Inside the grounds is the well-known Jardin Exotique. In my opinion this is the best view of the coast on the Côte d'Azur." Nic parked the car. "We walk from here."

She climbed out of the car and they started making their way around the stone village in the night air. It formed a circular pattern at the base of the castle. The old buildings had high stone walls while the narrow roadways were made of redbrick-centered stone. "Everything is so well restored, Nic!"

"It keeps the tourists coming."

"Well, this tourist is grateful."

"I love it here," he murmured. "No cars here. Only donkeys have the right of passage. This is the best time to be here, when there aren't so many tourists."

"I'm crazy about it, Nic. All of it!" She peeked in every nook and cranny, where small art galleries and tiny gift shops were hidden, infecting him with her unique brand of enthusiasm for everything. Climbing a set of steps, they came upon a shop displaying jewelry and women's scarves. The soft gray chiffon with circles of white caught his eye. He could see it on Laura and bought it.

"Here." He looped it around her neck. "This looks like you."

She felt the material with her hands before lifting her eyes to him. The urge to kiss her was killing him.

"You shouldn't have done this."

He shrugged his shoulders. "Why not? You bought me a bottle of wine. This is my Christmas gift to you, a small thing I hoped would bring you pleasure."

Her features looked pained before she averted her eyes. "You've given me more pleasure than you can imagine, Nic. Thank you," she whispered before moving ahead of him.

Laura was wrong about that. He could imagine pleasure with her beyond belief, but he had to tamp down his desire for her. The wife he'd loved could still be alive. Even if she wasn't, she needed to be found and laid to rest before he could think about anything else.

They followed the village trail that eventually led to a vista point with the whole Mediterranean coast sprawled at their feet. He waited to hear what she'd say.

Laura was quiet for a long while. Finally she spoke. "You were right. It's a sight I'll never forget. I can't think of another spot on earth more beautiful than this."

Nic could not think of a woman more breathtaking than the one standing in front of him.

"Nana would have come here with Maurice. Maybe their trip is on one of the DVDs I haven't looked at yet."

"It's possible." But he didn't want to talk about their grandparents. This night was for him and Laura, no one else.

"If you want to know the truth," she said in a tremulous voice, "this whole trip has changed my life. When I go home, I'll be leaving a part of my heart here."

The ache in her voice matched his longing for her. "Let's not talk about your going back to the States yet. I have an idea. Tonight why don't we stay in the little hotel we passed a minute ago?"

She spun around, visibly shocked.

"We'll each get a room with a seafront view.

You have to be here when the sun starts to come up in the morning. I'll set my watch alarm and we'll enjoy it together from one of our terraces. There's a faint lavender that emerges from the darkness and starts to turn to pink, bathing the coast in fantastic colors every great artist has tried to capture on canvas."

Laura stared at him. He could hear her mind turning it over. "We didn't bring anything with us."

"Besides ourselves?" His heart thumped in his chest. She hadn't said no. He held his breath. "No, we didn't, but does it matter? One night out of our lives?" Laura had to know what he was asking. They were running out of time. Meanwhile, Nic's' sorrow over her imminent departure was killing him. If they had to say goodbye, he wanted to do it here.

"No," she answered softly. "I'd love to stay here."

Adrenaline surged through his veins. "After we eat breakfast on the terrace, we'll go back to the villa. There'll be plenty of time to get ready and be at the attorney's office by ten."

She nodded.

Together they retraced their steps to the charming little hotel carved out of the rock. He arranged for two rooms side by side on the second floor, overlooking the water. He flicked her a glance. "There's coffee or tea in the rooms. Would you rather have something in addition sent up?"

"After that marvelous dinner I couldn't manage anything else, but thank you."

He took the keys and handed one to her before they ascended the circular staircase. "I'll come by in five minutes to say good-night."

Laura let herself inside and locked the door. She should have told Nic she wanted to go back to the villa, but when she thought of never seeing him again, she couldn't stand it. A sadness washed over her, so intense she felt sick.

At first her mind waged the inner argument that staying here in separate rooms wasn't any different than staying in the guest bedroom at his villa. Except that it *was* different.

Though the whole world might not know what

was going on, *she* knew. She'd fallen desperately in love with Nic. She wanted to be with him all the time, in every way. But he was Dorine's husband. Being here with him under these circumstances was wrong.

She couldn't do this!

In the next breath she bolted out the door and ran straight into his tall, hard body.

"Nic—" She recoiled from the contact.

His features looked drawn. "Let's go home. I saw guilt written in your eyes before you shut the door."

He knew her too well. "I—I'm sorry."

"No. I'm the one who's sorry for putting you in a compromising position."

"Don't forget I came with you."

"Nevertheless it won't happen again." She heard it in his voice. He meant it. "Do you need anything from the room?"

"Just my purse."

"Then get it and I'll meet you downstairs in the lobby."

Though she was relieved that they were leaving, another part of her cried out that she'd just ruined the night they could have had together away from everyone else. Before she changed her mind again, she grabbed her purse and hurried below to join him. Neither of them spoke as they walked along the trail to the car.

"Nic," she began once they were headed back to Nice, "I—"

"Don't say anything."

"I have to! We talked about this on the cruiser. I should have had the strength to tell you I wanted to go home after we said good-night to Yves." She lowered her head. "I won't deny I find you very attractive. I wanted tonight to go on and on. This has taken me by complete surprise. I thought Adam meant more to me than he does."

"Laura—" His voice rasped.

"No. Let me finish while I can. You're a red-blooded man. After three years without any news of your wife, you have every reason to want to be with another woman. But Yves confided in me that in all that time, you haven't been disloyal to Dorine's memory. That says more about the kind of honorable man you are than anything else I can think of. So I've made a decision.

"After we visit the attorney in the morning, I'm going to tell Maurice I need to get back to San Francisco. I know he wants to send me on the Valfort jet, so let's arrange for the boxes to be put on board and I'll fly out later tomorrow. He'll understand when I tell him that I need to get back to Mom, who needs my support. I must get home and deal with that situation before any more time passes."

She saw his hands tighten on the steering wheel. "Maurice will have a hard time letting you go."

"I'll stay in close touch with him. We'll video chat and talk on the phone. I love him and want him in my life. If he's up to it in a few months, I'll invite him to come and stay with me for a week at my condo."

A grimace marred Nic's features. He didn't comment. They rode the rest of the way in silence.

When they reached the villa, she turned to him. "I'll get my bag packed tonight so I'll be ready to go to the airport after we go to the at-torney's office tomorrow."

He didn't say anything, but she was relieved they were home. She hurried inside and ran straight to her room. After undressing, she took a shower, then packed everything except what she'd wear for the flight home.

Before she climbed under the covers, she picked up the scarf. This was all she would have of Nic to take home with her. Once the lights were out, she clutched it to her, remembering how it had felt when he'd put it around her neck. Their lips had only been a centimeter apart.

The memory was too much for her. Her need for him was too great. She turned over and bur-ied her face in the pillow until it was sopping wet.

When morning came, she saw herself in the bathroom mirror and moaned at her blotchy face. Her eyes were actually red from crying. It took a good hour to restore herself to some semblance of order.

After arranging her hair in a twist with one of her clips, she dressed in the tweed suit she'd worn when she'd first arrived in Nice. Some-how she managed to pull herself together. From a distance, the person standing in front of the mirror looked like the professional business-woman. But she'd never fool Nic.

As Laura walked through the house with her suitcase, she found him by the French doors talking on the phone. Their eyes met for a heart-pounding moment before she searched out Arlette to thank her for everything. Then she returned to the dining room and sat down to help herself to breakfast.

This would be her last meal with Nic. Every-thing she did with him today would be for the final time. She couldn't bear it, but somehow she had to find the strength.

This morning he'd put on a claret-red turtle-neck sweater and dark trousers. Combined with his black hair and hard-muscled physique, he couldn't have looked more dashing. To never see him again was something she couldn't com-prehend.

He clicked off and joined her. His features had taken on a chiseled cast. "That was the detective. He's learned nothing from Interpol and doesn't feel the answer lies with overseas team members. I told him about the conversation you and I had about the park. I've convinced him a search is worth doing—I told him money is no object. He has agreed to arrange for a massive ground search of Sophia Antipolis. He's hoping to get it underway within the next seven days."

She looked down at her roll. "The expense will be enormous, Nic."

"It'll be worth it. Even if nothing turns up, I will have done everything possible to find Dorine. I have you to thank for that."

Laura couldn't swallow for a minute. "I didn't do anything."

"Oh, but you did. I'd put aside the idea of searching the whole area a long time ago, feeling it would be futile. Then you talked to me about it. Even if it's been three years, you convinced me some kind of a clue could turn up. It's worth any amount of money and man-hours to find out."

Her eyes smarted with tears. "I'm going to pray they find something, Nic."

"Me, too," he whispered. "I plan to join them. Yves will help. So will my cousins."

For a number of reasons Laura couldn't stay to help in the search, but it didn't mean she didn't want to. For him to find closure would help him to really live again. "I'm so glad the detective is planning to organize it soon."

Nic glanced at his watch. "It's time we headed for the attorney's office in Nice."

She nodded. "I'll just get my purse."

Laura had put it on the dresser. As she reached for it, she noticed the scarf lying on the floor at the side of the bed. After a slight hesitation, she picked it up and draped it around her neck. She wanted him to know she loved it.

With the sun shining, she needed to put on her sunglasses to shield her red-rimmed eyes. Nic sent her a piercing glance as they drove out to the main road. It was as if he were telling her it was too late to hide anything from him. "I had that suit in mind when I saw the scarf."

"You have a discerning eye. It goes perfectly with it. I'll always treasure it." Her voice caught.

He reached out a hand to squeeze hers before

releasing it. "I phoned the pilot, who will have the jet fueled and ready to go any time after two. The storage company will deliver your boxes before takeoff."

"You always take care of everything." She crossed her legs restlessly. "Have you talked to Maurice this morning?"

"No. I thought we'd drop in on him at the château when we've finished our business with Monsieur Broussard. He's in the same firm with our family attorney and has spoken with him about your decision to will the property back to Maurice. There won't be any problem. Since you didn't take possession or sign anything yet, you won't have to pay taxes."

Laura groaned. "I forgot about those. A fine businesswoman I am."

"These were unusual circumstances."

The man seated next to her was a breed apart from other men. How was she going to get through the rest of her life without him?

"Nic—" She glanced over at him. "Do you think Maurice will be terribly hurt?"

"To be honest, I know he's so happy you came

to Nice in the first place, he'll be fine with your decision. After all, it was your grandmother who willed the summerhouse to you. He was only carrying out her wishes. In exchange he got himself the granddaughter he'd always wanted to know."

She bit the underside of her lip so hard it drew blood. "What do you think he'll do with it?"

"Before he makes any decision, I'm thinking of buying it."

Laura sat straight up. *"You?"*

He eyed her curiously. "Though I loved the château, the summerhouse was my fort when I was young."

"You're kidding!" she cried softly.

"Being that it was abandoned, it provided the perfect *endroit* for playing war with no one else around. Yves and I spent years there with our friends. It was my favorite place to be. I thought that when I grew up, I'd make enough money to buy it."

"That's so touching, Nic."

"Unfortunately because I thought of it as my own, it took me time to adjust to the idea that

Maurice decided to restore it so he could live there with Irene."

At this point Laura was totally fascinated. "Did Maurice know how you felt?"

"I doubt he knew that in refurbishing it, he'd robbed me of part of my boyhood delights. But after they moved in, they welcomed me to come any time. Irene always encouraged me to stay over whenever I felt like it, so it took away the sting."

"Until you found out he'd given it to my grand-mother. That would have hurt."

He shook his head. "By then I was all grown-up and liked her too much to be upset."

"Even though she willed it to the enemy?"

He flicked her a glance. "We know how that turned out, don't we," he said in a husky voice.

Her heart jumped. She'd fallen in love with the enemy.

Laura had no idea all this had been going on inside him. "If you bought it from Maurice, what would you do with it?"

"Live there."

She blinked. "But what about your villa?"

"I need to separate myself from the past. The villa was Dorine's idea from start to finish. Since her disappearance I've thought of moving, but haven't been able to settle on anything I've seen."

"Except for the summerhouse," she whispered.

"Yes."

"You don't think he'll move back in?"

"Frankly, I don't. It has too many memories for him. But if *I* lived there, he could come and go at will. I'd be near enough to help watch out for him. He's not getting any younger. Neither is Auguste. My parents already need additional help in the caretaking department."

"He loves you so much."

"It's mutual. I have a few ideas to convert the greenhouse in the back into a laboratory for my work. The light is exceptional. Since he had it remodeled, my siblings and cousins would all love the chance to buy it. If I tell Maurice I want it, he'll be fair and announce it to the family. Everyone will make a bid for it. Hopefully mine will come in higher than the other offers."

During their conversation they'd driven into the heart of Nice. Nic turned a corner and parked in front of an office building. "Let's get this over so you can spend the rest of the time with Grandfather before you fly away."

Fly away. That's what Laura would be doing in a few hours. She wondered if you could die from the pain of heartache.

Once they were inside the building, a secretary escorted them to a suite where Monsieur Broussard was waiting. Nic made the introductions before the brown-haired attorney asked them to be seated.

"I've been alerted to the particulars, Ms. Tate, and have all the papers here. It's your wish to will the property willed to you by your deceased grandmother to Maurice Valfort?"

"That's correct. I live and work in San Francisco, California. I couldn't be here enough or maintain it in order to warrant keeping it."

"I understand. What we'll do is issue a quit-claim deed. It will take about ten minutes. When you're ready to sign, I'll ask two of my colleagues to step inside and witness it."

"Wonderful."

"What is the full name of Maurice?"

"Maurice Sancerre Valfort," Nic supplied.

"Excellent."

Laura heard Nic's cell phone ring. He checked the caller ID before looking at her. "I need to take this call. It's Lieutenant Thibault."

She couldn't have been happier about it. "Go ahead."

"I'll be right back." He stepped out of the office.

If he hadn't gotten that call, she would have been forced to ask him to leave on some errand for her. This had worked out perfectly. The second he closed the door, she leaned forward. "Monsieur Broussard, while we're alone, I need to change something on the deed."

He lifted his head. "What do you mean?"

"I'm not willing the house to Maurice. It's going to go to someone else, but I don't want Maurice or Nic to know about it until it's signed, sealed and delivered."

His brows furrowed. "I don't understand."

"It's very simple. Since I own the house and

my grandmother told me I could do whatever I wanted with it, I've decided I'm going to give it to the one person who should have it."

"Who would that be?"

"Maurice's grandson, Nicholas Valfort. Nic watched out for his grandfather and my grandmother for years. As you know, the château is close to the summerhouse. Maurice lives in the château now. With Nic living in the summerhouse, they'd both be closer so Nic can help look after him. But we need to do this quickly before he comes back inside."

The older man had to digest it for a minute. "If you're certain."

"I've never been so certain of anything in my life." He needed to live in a place he'd always loved that wouldn't have the same reminders of Dorine.

"I'd like you to send all the paperwork to Maurice. While you're finishing up, I need to write a note." She reached in her purse for small notebook and tore out a sheet. "When I've finished, will you ask your secretary to type up what I've written and put it with the documents?

Maurice can be the one to let Nic know what I've done." The attorney nodded. "Do you swear you'll keep this a secret until after it's been delivered to Maurice?"

He eyed her for a long time. "I swear."

"Thank you. You have no idea what this means to me. Nic is the most wonderful man alive. This gift is going to make him so happy you can't imagine."

A faint smile broke out on Broussard's face. "Do you have any concept of the value of that property? Some would be willing to pay a king's ransom for it."

"I don't care about that."

"Then you're a very generous woman."

"A thankful woman," she corrected him. "Because of Nic, I was united with the grandfather I never knew. He, in turn, helped me to know the grandmother who'd been lost to me. I owe Nic a debt of gratitude I can never repay. He flew my grandmother's body back to California and let me know she'd left me a gift. It's beyond price."

If she wasn't mistaken, the lawyer's eyes

"Thank you."

It wasn't any too soon. Suddenly Nic swept back in the room. Before long the transaction had been completed. The notaries signed the documents. Laura's signatures came last and Nic was none the wiser about the transfer or her personal note, thank heaven.

When they reached the car, Nic helped her inside and they left for the château.

"What did the detective want?"

He looked over at her. "To let me know the whole department is behind the search. He's worked tirelessly on this case and is anxious to solve it. While I was out in the hall, I heard from Maurice. He's asked us to meet at the summerhouse, where he has one more surprise waiting. It's your bon voyage gift."

"Do you know what it is?"

"No."

She laughed gently. "There's never a dull moment with him. No wonder my grandmother was so crazy about him." After that comment he drove faster than usual and whizzed through the estate to the summerhouse.

Pain of a new kind had a stranglehold on her. It wouldn't be long before she was gone. She didn't know if she could take it. There was no way they could make small talk right now. When they reached the house, she got out of the car the minute he stopped and hurried inside without waiting for him.

"Et voilà, mes enfants." Maurice hugged both of them. "I'm so glad you're here. Come and sit down. I have something to show you that I couldn't find until the other day. I had it put on a DVD immediately. It was in my old valise, the one I was using at the time Irene and I got married."

His excitement was so contagious, they did his bidding and waited until he started the machine. "When Irene and I decided to get married, I asked the concierge at the hotel where I was staying to find someone who would film our wedding."

Laura was thunderstruck as he started the DVD and Maurice and her grandmother suddenly appeared on the screen. "You look like movie stars!" she cried.

Maurice nodded with tears in his eyes. "She was a vision in that white suit."

"You look just like her in that suit you're wearing," Nic murmured.

Nic...

Unable to sit still, she got up to move closer. "In that dark suit you're so handsome, my grandmother couldn't have helped but be in love with you, *Gran'père.* I never saw two people who looked so happy."

"For that day, we were divinely happy."

Even amid all the fighting that surrounded their union.

She had to blink away the tears.

The rest of the film showed them coming out of the building and getting in a limo. More video followed of the two of them eating at a restaurant she didn't recognize. They kissed several times for the camera. It was so sweet, so loving.

When it came to an end, Laura walked over

and put her arms around him. "You've discovered a treasure."

"I want you to have it." He sounded choked up.

"No. You've given me everything else. This is for you. Now you can watch it whenever you like and remember that joyous time. The next time I come to Nice, I'll watch it with you and then we'll take walks together."

He got to his feet. "I know you have to go, but it's hard."

"For me, too," she admitted and kissed his cheek. "Is there anything I can do for you before I leave?"

His moist brown eyes studied her. "You can decide to stay here. This is your home now."

No, it isn't, but don't tempt me.

"There's nothing I'd love more, but I can't and you know why. Remember, I'll come for visits. In the meantime, tell you what—I'll call you every day to get your advice on my marketing schemes. What better tutor than the man who put Valfort Hotels on the map!"

"You flatter me, but that was *my* grandfather."

"According to the letters Nana wrote me, you were known as the Valfort who brought the hotel business into the twenty-first century. With your help, I might make it to CEO one day."

"Is that what you want?"

She swallowed hard. "I need a goal." How else was she going to survive her life unless she had a goal that drove her day and night? "Why not rise to the top? It might be interesting to be the first woman on the board."

"If you're that ambitious, why not move to France and work for me? You're practically a Valfort, after all."

Laura cocked her head. "Is that a serious job offer?"

"What if it were?" Maurice fired back. "Would you seriously consider it? Don't answer that question yet. See what happens after you get back to San Francisco, then call me and we'll discuss it."

The authority in his voice gave her a glimpse of the steel behind the charm. It was that same steel she'd heard in Nic's voice. She'd never forget the moment when he'd first grasped her arms and made her promise not to tell his grandfather what she'd just told him about her family's lies.

"I promise to call you." She kissed his cheek. "Now I'm afraid we have to be going."

He looked at Nic. "I'll drive to the airport with you to see you off."

Laura reached for her purse, then looped her arm through Maurice's. They walked out of the house together. Nic went ahead of them and opened the back door of his car for his grandfather. Laura took advantage of the moment to get in the front seat without his help. The less touching, the less torment.

"Nic? En route could you stop by a store that sells picture frames? I'll only be a minute."

"Bien sûr."

They drove through the estate to the main road. After Nic parked in front of a shop so Laura could run her errand, they headed for the airport. She looked around one last time. Talk about pain.

She didn't think Nic would ever get answers

about Dorine, so it might be four more years before he was free again. Laura had reconciled herself to the fact that it might be that long before she could have a relationship with him, *if* he still wanted one with her. That would put her at thirty-one and him at thirty-seven. But it didn't matter, because she'd wait twenty years for him if she had to.

The truck from the storage company had already arrived on the tarmac and was loading boxes in the rear of the jet with the steward's help. Nic pulled up next to it. While he went around for her suitcase in the trunk, she got out and opened Maurice's door.

"I forgot to give this to you at the house." She pulled a small photograph of herself from her wallet and fit it into the little frame she'd purchased. "This was taken a month ago at a marketing conference."

Maurice studied it for a moment before putting it in his pocket. *"Merci, ma chère fille."*

"God bless you, *Gran'père.* Don't get on the plane with me. This is hard enough." She gave him a huge hug.

"Promise you'll phone me the second you've arrived in San Francisco. I have to know you got there safely."

"Of course I will." Tears blurred her eyes as she moved toward the jet and hurried up the stairs.

Nic followed her on board with her suitcase and put it up in the rack. He noted with satisfaction she was still wearing the scarf.

"That little photo meant the world to Maurice."

Those iridescent-blue eyes stared up at him. "I came to Nice totally unprepared for what I'd find here. I'll send him more."

He sucked in his breath and moved closer to her. "How soon do you think you'll be back to visit Maurice?"

A tiny nerve was throbbing in the base of her creamy throat. "With my travel schedule, not for a long time." Moistening her lips nervously she asked, "Did the detective tell you how soon he's starting the ground search?"

"January 2."

"The day after New Year's. That's not very far away."

"It can't come soon enough for me."

"For me, either." Her voice throbbed. He realized that was a big admission on her part. "I want your pain to end."

They stared at each other. "Hopefully because of the resources I've put behind it, there will be a big turnout of volunteers."

"If you ran ads over the television, the word would spread like wildfire."

"I'm not sure if the police will do that, but they have their methods when it comes to a search like this."

"Of course."

His lungs had locked tight. "I'm going to miss you, Laura."

She averted her eyes. "The three of us have been through a life-changing experience together. Nothing will ever be the same again, not for any of us."

He was fast losing control. "Do you have any comprehension of how hard it is to let you go?"

Her body had started trembling. He could see it. "Don't you know it's killing me to leave? Please go, Nic. I can't take any more."

The steward made an appearance. "The captain is ready to take off."

She paled visibly.

This was torture of a different kind than Nic had ever known before. "Have a safe flight, Laura."

Nic had to get out of there now or he'd never leave. He wheeled around and exited the jet. Maurice had gotten in the front seat of the car and was waiting for him. Forcing himself to slide behind the wheel, he started the engine and took off. By the time they reached the main road, the Valfort jet had risen in the sky and would be out of sight any minute now.

A groan escaped him he couldn't prevent.

"I feel the same way, *mon fils*. What do you say we go back to the summerhouse and finish the Pinot she gave me for Christmas? I believe there's enough to help us get through the night."

Nic shook his head. "If your doctor could hear you talk…"

"If my doctor knew how we felt right now, he'd give us his blessing and join us."

CHAPTER EIGHT

After landing in San Francisco, Laura texted Maurice to let him know she was home safe and sound. A phone call would have wakened him. As for Nic, she didn't dare contact him and start anything. Tomorrow she'd ring Maurice, who would communicate any news to his grandson.

Once she was back in her condo and settled, she phoned her mom to let her know she was back. Then she called Adam and had the conversation with him that ended their relationship. He wanted to come over, but she told him no. After explaining she wasn't the same woman who'd left, he quieted down.

"When I went to Nice, certain things happened that have changed my life."

"This has to do with your grandmother."

"Yes. I got answers, but that isn't all. My grandmother's husband has a grandson, Nic

Valfort. I stayed at his villa while I was in Nice. He was the one who came on the Valfort jet with my grandmother's body."

"Are you telling me you got involved with him?"

"I didn't mean to. It just happened."

"Are you saying you slept with him?"

"No. Not even close."

"But you wanted to."

Her heart was in her throat. "He's a married man." In the next few minutes she told Adam about Dorine and the ground search that would be happening after New Year's.

"You're in love with him."

"Whatever it is I feel, it's strong enough that I can't go on seeing you."

"You mean you're going to wait for him?"

"Yes."

"Has he asked you to wait?"

"No."

"If he never finds her, how do you know he'll want you in four more years?"

"I don't, but while I feel like this about him, I can't be with another man."

"You know all this in a week's time?"

"Yes. Forgive me."

"My hell, I can't believe this is happening."

"This thing that happened was out of my control." From the first moment she'd met Nic in the Holden headquarters foyer, she'd been drawn to him. "I'm so sorry. You have no idea how terrible I feel. I would never deliberately hurt you. You must know that."

"I'm not sure I know anything anymore! You've just smashed all my dreams!" He clicked off first. It was better this way.

With that hurdle taken care of, Laura showered and changed into her robe. Later she went through her business emails and checked for any emergencies, but it seemed her assistant had taken care of everything.

She paced the floor. It was Nic she wanted. When she thought of him, she couldn't breathe. The next best thing to being with him was watching a video of him.

Along with the first video she'd seen of him at fourteen, she'd grabbed half a dozen of the DVDs and packed them in her suitcase. She hadn't looked at any of those yet. He'd probably be in one or two of them. The boxes containing all her treasures had been picked up by the movers who'd met the jet. They'd be delivered tomorrow. Tonight she couldn't wait to watch the ones that were handy. She put the disk from the top of the pile in the machine. Finally she could get comfortable on the couch and immerse herself in her grandmother's gifts that kept on giving.

The screen showed an old church on a busy street lined with trees.

"My darling Laura—Maurice and I are in Grenoble. Today is Nic's wedding to Dorine Soulis."

Laura gasped.

"We attended the Mass, but came outside so we could take a picture as they walk out the doors. You can see the families assembled on the steps. It was a beautiful wedding. She's petite and so chic. I think she makes the most adorable bride."

Adorable was the word Laura had used in describing Nic's wife. Suddenly the doors opened and there stood an impossibly handsome, smiling Nic in a black tux with his arm around Dorine's waist. Dressed in white with a flowing veil, she looked like a dark-haired angel.

"They're leaving for a honeymoon in Spain. They plan to be gone two weeks. Maurice and I will miss them, so we've decided we're going to take a trip to Australia. I'll make another video when we get there. By the time we get back, they will have returned to their new home in Nice. It's not that far from us. She found them the perfect villa. Dorine is quite the decorator."

The camera moved closer and showed Nic helping Dorine into the limo. While she was smiling at everyone, Nic lowered his head and kissed her fully, to the joy of the crowd. Laura could hear the clapping and cheers from family and friends.

But she couldn't stand another second and shut the video off with the remote. Pain stabbed her repeatedly until she felt faint. Nic's darling bride was no more. All that happiness wiped out one afternoon on her lunch hour, and Nic still didn't have answers.

Beside herself with grief for him—for Dorine and what horrors she must have suffered, for the horrors Nic would have conjured up wondering what had happened to her—Laura fell sideways on the couch and sobbed until oblivion took over.

Jet lag must have caught up with her, because she didn't wake until she heard her doorbell ring the next morning. By prearrangement the movers were here and she'd slept in her robe all night!

She buzzed them through, then stumbled to the door and opened it to let them in, knowing she looked a wreck. They put everything in the living room. Once she'd signed the receipt, they left.

Laura sank back down on the couch, burying her face in her hands. So many emotions were bombarding her she could barely function. After seeing the radiant look on Nic's face in that video, a look that would never come again, she was thankful she'd flown home before she'd done something she'd regret through eternity.

Laura had provided a few days of distraction

for Nic's grief. Because she was Irene's grand-daughter and he was Maurice's grandson, they'd both been caught off guard by the unwitting attraction. But that's all it was on his part. An attraction. It couldn't be anything else and never would be. That man had loved his wife and still did.

There was a love song with the lyrics, "If it takes the rest of our lives, I will wait for you." It was one of Laura's favorites. She'd told Adam she'd wait four years for Nic, but that was before she'd seen the video.

Nic wasn't hers to wait for…

The video had made her mind up for her.

If there was to be any visiting from here on out, Maurice would have to come to her while he was still healthy enough to travel. She'd already dismissed the idea of working for him. That would be madness.

As she'd told him, with a lot of hard work she was aiming for CEO of Holden Hotels, like her grandfather Richard. That would be a goal to help her forget there was such a thing as a personal life.

But while she sat there feeling utterly helpless and wishing there were something she could do to help Nic, an idea came to her that wouldn't let go of her. She jumped off the couch and hurried to her bedroom. He would never have to know about it.

In the next hour she put through a call to police headquarters in Nice, asking to speak to someone who spoke English and could tell her about the Valfort search.

In a minute someone came on the line. "Yes? This is Jean-Jacques, one of the coordinators."

"Oh, good. I'm a friend of the Valfort family. I understand you're putting a massive search group together to look for the missing wife of Nicholas Valfort starting on the second. I've never been trained for this sort of thing, but I'd like to help in any way I can, both physically and monetarily."

"*Très bien!* We can use volunteers who will help feed the rescuers coming and going off shift."

"I can do that. Just give me an address and a time and I'll be there."

"*Excellent.* We are working in grids. The address I'm giving you will be in the north end of the park. There will be signs to help you find the exact spot." The man gave her the specific information. "Bring warm clothing, boots and gloves. The forecast calls for eighty percent rain over those days. We could be working through three or four nights."

There hadn't been a cloud in the sky during Laura's stay there. She couldn't believe the weather would turn like that. "Understood. Thank you."

After she'd hung up, she called the airlines and scheduled a flight to Nice on New Year's Day, two days from now. Once that was done, she got on the internet and found information for several hotels near the entrance to Sophia Antipolis. She booked a room at one of them and arranged for a rental car.

After thinking it over, she decided that when she reached Nice and was given an orientation with the other volunteers, she would make arrangements with a local restaurant to supply food and coffee.

There wasn't enough she could do for Nic. Sitting here in San Francisco feeling helpless was untenable. If the search didn't produce anything, at least she would have the satisfaction of knowing she'd shown her love for him in the only way she knew how.

Relieved to be doing something constructive at last, Laura showered and got ready to drive over to her mom's. The issue with her aunt Susan was all that occupied Jessica's thoughts right now. Finding the right psychiatrist was crucial.

Later in the day she'd run to headquarters and tell Dean about the emergency that meant she'd be leaving the country again. Her assistant would have to reschedule her travel plans to the various hotels around the state. The marketing ideas were important, but they took a backseat to the search for Dorine.

Nic had been in prison too long. If his wife's case could be solved, it would add ten years to Maurice's life, too. Maybe Laura was being fanciful, but she'd like to think her nana would be helping out from the other side. Irene had loved Nic, too.

* * *

Nic was still working alone in his office at seven on New Year's Eve when his cell rang. He checked the caller ID and clicked on. "Gran'père? I thought you were at the family party at the château."

"I am, but something has come up. Where are you?"

"I'm finishing some work at the office. I'll join you eventually."

"Quit whatever you're doing and meet me at the summerhouse."

Nic's black brows knit together. "You mean now?"

"Yes. Hurry."

"Are you all right?"

"Of course, but we need to talk!"

"I'm leaving now."

He turned off lights and walked out to the parking lot. Something told Nic the attorney had couriered the documents about the quit-claim deed to his grandfather and he was upset about it. Laura had filled the days for his grandfather while she'd been here, but now that she was gone, Maurice hadn't been able to throw off his depression. By willing the house back to him, she'd made his outlook worse.

Ever since Nic had watched Laura fly out of his life, he'd lost sleep and his emotions had been too raw to be around other people. It was a good thing his office had been closed over the holidays. Even between working on company business in solitude and putting together a search team with the detective, he'd barely managed not to go off the rails.

The lights of the summerhouse beckoned. He pulled up next to the Renault, but almost dreaded stepping inside because Laura wasn't there. Nothing was the same now that she'd gone. *"Enfin,"* his grandfather called out when Nic entered the living room. The older man held a sheaf of papers in his hand, just as Nic had suspected. "Take a look at this!" He handed him the top sheet.

"I already know what Laura did."

Maurice squinted at him. "You do?"

"Yes. Don't be upset with her, *Gran'père.* You've found out she's a wonderful, unselfish woman just like her grandmother. She could no more take your house with its memories away from you than she could stop breathing."

"But she *did* take it away from me."

Nic thought he hadn't heard his grandfather correctly. "Say that again."

"You'd better look at this sheet."

Puzzled at this point, Nic reached for it. The quitclaim deed had been filled out with another name. *Nicholas Honfleur Valfort.*

"She willed the house to *you.*"

As memories of a certain conversation with Laura flashed through his mind, the evidence before his eyes rendered him speechless.

"She also left this note. In the state you're in, I'd better read it to you. 'My dear Maurice— Nana told me I could do what I wanted with the summerhouse. So many happy memories reside there because of the love between the two of you. But I know of other happy memories of a Frenchman whose early youth was enriched because of the years he played in the old greenhouse and ruled his own fort.

"'Nothing would please me more than to know he can call it his own again. No one deserves a little piece of happiness more than your magnificent grandson, who once upon a time was a carefree boy Irene loved like her own.'"

Maurice handed him the note. After clearing his throat he said, "When you've pulled yourself together, come to the château and join the party, *mon fils.* Your parents have assembled family and friends from afar to be of help to you in your search after New Year's Day. The first thing we're going to do is say a special prayer that your agony will end soon."

Long after his grandfather had left the house, Nic stood there, incredulous over what Laura had done. His mind went back to something Irene had said in the video. Her words had never spoken to him the way they did at this moment.

You can experience a profound love more than once in this life, as Maurice and I found out. Otherwise what would be the point of existence?

January 4

Portable tables with a protective canopy had been set up all around the technology park to serve as a rest stop for hot food and first aid. Laura and a college guy named Patrick, who was on crutches, had been manning the station from the get-go. They gave out sandwiches and coffee from several bistros and restaurants. She'd funded everything from her bank account, which included paying the drivers in the trucks who made continuous deliveries.

The light rain had pretty well kept up the whole time, forcing her to pull the hood of her water-resistant Windbreaker over her head. But on the third night of the search, it finally stopped long enough to give the volunteers working the grid in her sector some relief.

Every so often a patrol officer would come by for coffee. She'd listen as they spoke with other officers on their radios, then she'd ask for a translation. They were counting on the dogs from the canine corps units to turn up something, but nothing had been found yet. It was a laborious, exhausting process for those walking in lines following a set pattern so that every inch of ground was covered. Their sacrifice was carried out in less than favorable conditions, but everyone there was committed.

Her heart swelled to see the dedication. She could only imagine how Nic felt to know so many had turned out to search for Dorine. From what she could see, it looked as though a small portion of the city had come to lend their assistance. Cars, trucks and buses were parked everywhere. The tragedy that had befallen Nic and his wife was everyone's tragedy.

All the while she gave out food and drink, she was aware that Nic was somewhere in the park, walking the lines with his family and friends. Knowing Maurice, he would be waiting at the château with his brother for any word.

By noon of the fourth day, word circulated that the search would be called off within the hour. The light rain had started up again. In the unnatural silence that followed the announcement, Laura's spirits sank to think this entire effort might not have produced results, but they'd had to try and no one wanted to give up. Though it was time for her to go back to the hotel, she couldn't leave yet.

"I'll stay until it's over, Patrick. You've done your part. Go home and get some sleep."

"I couldn't do that. I'll wait it out to the end. If my fiancée had gone missing, I'd move heaven and earth to find her, too."

She handed him a cup of coffee. "You took the words out of my mouth. You're a good person."

"So are you. Not every tourist would interrupt her vacation to help."

Laura moaned for Nic's pain while they prepared to feed the last shift coming in. As she was putting fresh sandwiches out on plates, she heard voices coming from far off. Lots of shouting. The sound grew in strength to a roar. Her heart jumped to her throat. She looked at Patrick. "They've found something!"

For the next few minutes Laura couldn't breathe while they waited for word. Pretty soon a patrol car came by.

"I'll find out." Patrick hurried over on his crutches to the officer. When he turned and moved toward Laura, she could tell he was excited. "The dogs found a grave with two bodies. Through certain physical evidence, one of them was positively identified as Dorine Valfort. They've called off the search."

A cry of thanksgiving poured out of Laura. *Nic...Nic...it's over, my love.*

He had to be overcome with so many emotions. Exquisite relief that she'd been found, of course, but now he would have to deal with the reality of what his wife's trauma had been and all she must have gone through, plus the dawning realization that all hope that she could return to him was lost. This was a time for mourning and Laura feared for Nic. He could go into a depression of a different kind and might not come out of it for who knew how long.

Laura started putting the food and cups back in the cartons for the trucks to haul away, but her hands were shaking. Filled with questions about the unidentified other body, she did her part to clean up, then hurried to her car. This news would be all over the media. She raced back to her hotel to check out and drive to the airport.

Nic's new grieving process was just beginning along with the families'. They would have a funeral, followed by more rivers of sorrow, to endure now that they could give in to their emotions.

The thing to do was fly home and immerse herself in work. Laura had never known Dorine, but she mourned her death, too. One day Laura might see Nic again, but probably not, because he was sensitive to the feelings of Dorine's family and his own. There'd be talk otherwise. His life needed to go in an entirely different direction now.

CHAPTER NINE

March 3

"Nic?"

"*Oui,* Robert?"

"Lieutenant Thibault is here. He says it's important."

"Tell him to come in." Nic jumped up from his office chair. He'd almost lost his mind waiting for news.

The detective entered his office. "The case is now officially closed, Nic. The Sûreté tracked down the man responsible. He's now in custody in Rouen. They got a confession. It'll be all over the evening news."

"Thank God." This was the information that had sprung his prison door at last.

"The lowlife and his wife worked at the Valfort Hotel in the Old Town. After resigning their jobs, they kidnapped your wife to collect a ransom. When they followed her from her office, they created a diversion so she would stop.

"While his wife held a gun on your wife, he drove Dorine's car into town and left it. Then he came back. But upon his return he found your wife dead in their car. His wife claimed there'd been a struggle and the gun had gone off by accident. In an angry rage because everything had gone wrong, he shot his wife and dug a grave for them that night before disappearing."

The news that Dorine hadn't suffered long before she was killed went a long way to bring Nic peace, but he needed to be alone. "Thank you, Lieutenant."

Once the detective left, Nic told Robert he was going home. When he reached the villa, he told Jean and Arlette he needed his privacy.

After they retired for the night, he went into the bedroom he'd shared with Dorine and collapsed on the bed. Great sobs shook his body. If he ate or drank, he didn't remember it. Three days later his grandfather walked in on him.

"I don't pretend to know the deep suffering

you've gone through, *mon fils,* but I do know Dorine is in heaven and happy. She's been there over three years and wants you to be happy, too."

Nic turned over on his back, looking at Maurice through red-rimmed eyes. "How terrified she must have been."

"Yes. But how moved she must have been to hear all the wonderful things said about her at the funeral, especially the outpouring of love from her honorable husband."

"Don't ever call me honorable."

"Why? Because you lost your heart to Irene's granddaughter during your Gethsemane? Want to know a secret? I lost my heart to her too. That dear girl helped both of us keep it together at the darkest moment of our lives. Now it's time to get on with living and put all the pain, all the guilt and all the suffering away. It's time to move into the summerhouse and dream new dreams."

Nic phoned Robert. "You're going to have to run the office for a while, because I'm leaving for California within the hour. I'll let you know when I'll be back."

On his way to the villa he phoned the pilot to get the jet ready. After he'd packed some clothes and was on his way to the airport, he phoned Maurice and gave him the news. "I'm flying to San Francisco."

"It's about time, *mon fils.*"

Long past time, was more like it Nic mused as he entered Holden headquarters the next day. It was two in the afternoon. When he saw the security guard in the foyer, it was like déjà vu.

"I'm here to see the marketing manager, Laura Tate."

"I'm sorry, but this is her first day of vacation, sir."

Nic felt as if he'd been punched in the gut. "For how long?"

"A week."

"Thank you." He turned on his heel and went back out to the limo. Maybe she hadn't left yet town yet. He'd try her condo. When he entered the foyer, he had to buzz her suite. If she didn't answer, then he'd phone her mother and find out her destination.

He was about to walk away when he heard her voice. "Yes?"

Beyond elated she was home he said, "I thought you were on vacation."

There was such a long silence, he wondered if she'd even heard him. Then, *"Nic?"* The joy in that one word would live with him all his life. "Is it really you?"

His eyes closed tightly for a moment. "Why don't you let me in and find out?"

"I'm on the second floor," she said in a tremulous voice. "Just take the stairs and I'm around the corner, number six."

He heard the click of the inner door, then hurried through and took the stairs three at a time. She met him when he'd reached the top step.

"Nic—" Her crystal-blue gaze played over him, blazing with a hunger to match his own. Deep in his soul he sensed nothing had changed between them. If anything, their love had deepened. "I've imagined this a thousand times in my dreams. I was afraid I might never see you again. I—I can't believe you're here." Her voice faltered.

"Invite me in and I'll convince you."

She backed into the condo, never taking her eyes off him. He shut the door behind him.

"I've done my grieving, Laura. Dorine is at peace now, and so am I. We can catch up on everything later, but right now I don't want to talk. I just want to hold you."

In the next instant she ran into his arms, enveloping him with her intoxicating fragrance. He crushed her beautiful body against his. The reality of her hadn't begun to sink in yet. He needed more of her, wanted all of her. He wanted too much all at once. He was still trying to get it through his mind and heart she was here with him at last. No barriers to keep them apart.

Impatient for everything denied them, he picked her up and carried her over to the couch. She clung to him with a hungry moan as he followed her down. He was desperate for this closeness while he kissed the mouth he craved over and over again.

They lost track of time trying to merge, but no kiss, no matter how long and deep, could satisfy his need. He would never be able to get enough of her. Their legs tangled while his hands became enmeshed in her silvery-gold hair.

"I love you, *mon amour.* I've wanted to say that since Christmas Eve, when we watched the video in my den. You changed my world."

Laura covered his face with kisses, thrilling him as he hadn't thought possible. "I knew I'd fallen in love with you before I climbed out of the limousine that first day. I love you so much I hurt to the palms of my hands." She sought his mouth again with the kind of passion that was burning him alive.

"We need to get married. Since you willed it to me, I'm thinking the summerhouse. A small, intimate ceremony. We'll make our home there after we come home from our honeymoon."

"I think I'm dying of happiness."

"Tomorrow we'll fly back to Nice. You'll have to handle your corporate job long-distance. I don't ever want to be separated from you again.

These past months…" His voice cracked. He couldn't finish.

"Hush, darling. It's over. All of it." She pressed his head to her chest. For a little while they both let go of their emotions and wept. While she rocked him, she kissed his hair and told him how she'd flown to Nice to help in the search.

"You were there?"

"Yes. I heard the noise and the barks of the dogs."

"I can't believe it. You never told me or Maurice."

"No. That was your private time. I knew how much you loved Dorine. I saw the video of your wedding after I got back to San Francisco. That's why I didn't come near you at the time, or phone you. I knew I had to wait and hope that like our grandparents, who were given a second chance at happiness, one day you might grow to love me enough to come for me."

Laura's love astounded and humbled him.

A week later the family priest officiated at the late-afternoon wedding ceremony in the living room of the summerhouse. The first person to embrace Laura after she and Nic became man and wife was Maurice.

In a croaking voice he said, "Little did I know when I had to say goodbye to my beloved wife for the last time, I'd be welcoming a new Madame Valfort into the family. My own beautiful granddaughter."

She let out a gentle laugh. "Don't get me started on the tears, *Gran'père,* or I'll never stop and my brand-new husband won't know what to do with me."

Nic's strong arms went around her waist from behind. He was never far from her. "If you believe that, then you don't know me at all," he whispered into her neck, thrilling her. Her cream-colored lace suit, which she'd chosen rather than a wedding dress, made it easy for him to pull her against him. She'd wanted simplicity.

It was a day of intense happiness. Her gaze took in her mom and Yves, who both broke off talking to hug them. Yves had videotaped the wedding and had also volunteered to drive her mother back to the villa. She would stay the night before he drove her to the airport to return to San Francisco.

All of Nic's family had assembled and welcomed her as one of their own. What Maurice and Irene hadn't been able to enjoy had come back to bless Laura and Nic in profound ways. Two families were healing. Her aunt Susan was in therapy in San Francisco. Laura had a feeling her grandmother was looking down and smiling.

Nic tugged on a strand of her blond hair, which she'd left long the way he loved it. "I don't know about you, but I'm ready to leave."

She turned in his arms. "We can't go yet. You *know* we can't."

"Then kiss me so I can stand it."

In this mood Nic was irresistible. She raised up to press a kiss to his lips, but he took advantage and gave her a husband's kiss, hot with desire. Heat swarmed her cheeks because everyone would have noticed. She burrowed against him for a moment to gain her composure. "Be good, darling."

"I'm being as good as I can for a new bride-groom."

"No, you're not."

"But you love me."

"You *have* to know that by now. I've been living to become your wife."

"I want more proof."

Her pulse raced. "I promise you'll have it later tonight."

"Don't you know I have a voracious appetite for you and want it for the rest of our lives?"

They heard someone tapping on a Champagne glass. Flushed with love and desire, she turned in his arms. Maurice's brother, Auguste got to his feet with difficulty.

"I'd like to propose a toast to Nicholas and his bride. Everything good started to happen the day she flew in to Nice. I wish we had gathered like this for my brother and Irene. Our family should have celebrated their marriage and I'm sorry about that. But we can celebrate new beginnings with the new generation of Valforts. May Nic and Laura be happy and fruitful."

"To new beginnings," everyone joined in.

Nic's arms held her tighter. "Did you hear that, *mon amour?* It's time to go and fulfill every wish. Our bags are packed and waiting for us in the car."

She blushed again. "Where are you taking me?"

"It's not far, believe me." He reached for her hand and pulled her toward the foyer with him. Everyone rushed forward as they slipped out the front door to the car. Yves kept filming them as Nic helped her inside.

"Let's have a kiss," he called out, but Nic didn't respond.

Surprised, maybe even a little hurt, she lowered the window. "*À bientôt, Gran'père.* I love you. See you soon."

"Take your time," he called back. "There's only one honeymoon."

In another minute Nic had started the car and they pulled away. He grabbed hold of her hand. "Before you leap to the wrong conclusion, I had two reasons for not kissing you just then. Dorine and I saw Maurice's video of our wedding after we got home from our honeymoon. When I realized you'd seen it, too, I didn't want you having to make comparisons that could hurt y—"

"Don't say any more." She cut him off and squeezed his hand. "I love you for being so sensitive to my feelings. I'm afraid I love you too much."

"If you want to know my second reason, it's because I almost devoured you in front of our guests after the ceremony. To be honest, I didn't trust myself not to do the same thing again given the chance."

"If we're talking truths, I never trusted myself with you from the moment you picked me up at the airport in Nice."

"Ours was a trial of fire from the beginning."

She nodded. "Thank heaven that part is over. Do you swear we don't have much farther to go? I don't think I can stand to be this far apart from you any longer."

"Do you recognize this highway?"

She looked around and let out a half squeal. "You're taking me back to Eze—"

"This time I only booked one room. Just remember that after we get there, I won't let you out of my bed, let alone my sight."

"You think I feel any different?"

Once they reached the parking area, he grabbed their bags and they walked the trail to the little hotel.

"The night is so glorious, Nic."

"Balmy, just the way I like it."

The concierge greeted them and handed Laura the card key. Her body trembled with anticipation as they ascended the stairs to the next floor. She opened the door for them. This was so different from last time. For a moment she wondered if this was really happening.

"It's really happening," Nic murmured and put down the bags. He knew her so well he'd read her mind. After he opened the glass door to let in the night air, he turned to her. "Come here to me, my love."

The second she walked into his arms, she knew pleasure beyond anything in this life. They took their time getting to know each other in ways she hadn't even dreamed about. Nic was such a beautiful man. To think he was her husband. His possession of her was to die for.

But she didn't die. She was vibrantly alive and sought the rapture of fulfillment he gave her again and again. Toward morning he fell asleep. She lay at his side and watched him as the lavender tint he'd told her about illuminated the sky. Minute by minute the color changed to the indescribable pink he'd talked about.

The magical hues filled the room, bringing out the Gallic features that made him such a gorgeous man. She gasped quietly in awe, but he heard her. His eyelids opened. The gray of his irises between his black lashes had turned crystalline in the early-morning light.

"What is it, *ma belle?*"

Laura loved it when he called her that. She leaned over to kiss his mouth. "Nothing's wrong. I simply felt like looking at you. No woman could be as lucky as I am. I'm hoping that one day soon we'll have a baby. It won't matter if it's a boy or a girl, because either way, they'll have the Valfort traits and qualities."

He kissed the palm of her hand. "Don't forget the Holden genes."

She smiled. "While I was getting ready for the wedding, Mother said you're the most sinfully handsome man she ever saw. I thought the same thing the first time I laid eyes on you, but I've never heard her express herself like that before."

"Sometime you'll have to ask Yves what I said about you." Her heart thudded in reaction. He raised up on one elbow. His eyes radiated excitement. "You honestly want a baby soon?"

Suddenly she felt anxious. "Don't *you?*"

"Now that I've got you, I want it all."

"If I was pregnant right now, would you mind?"

"Mind?" He pulled her on top of him. "How can you even ask me that?"

"Because we didn't ever really talk about it, but last night we didn't take precautions."

"So you're not on the Pill?"

"No. I've never slept with any man, so I didn't need to be."

A cry of joy escaped his throat. "So I could have made you pregnant during the night?"

"Yes. You have no idea how much I want your baby. I want us to be a real family. You're going to make the most wonderful father."

Suddenly he rolled her over so he was looking down at her. "I don't want you to move. We're going to stay in this room for the next couple of days. I'll order breakfast, lunch and dinner for us. In between meals we're going to be busy doing what I love doing best with you. Have I told you yet what a wonderful lover you are? You're the light of my life. I love you, *mon amour. Je t'aime,*" he cried, burying his face in her hair.

Laura's joy was full. She held the world in her arms and sang a certain song to him she'd memorized because of that night.

"Let's dance the old-fashioned way, my love. I want you to stay in my arms, skin against skin. Let me feel your heart, don't let any air in. Come close where you belong. Let's hear our secret song and dance in the old-fashioned way. Won't you stay in my arms? We'll discover higher highs we never knew before, if we just close our eyes and dance around the floor. It makes me love you more."

"Laura—"

* * * * *

MILLS & BOON®
Large Print – March 2015

A VIRGIN FOR HIS PRIZE
Lucy Monroe

THE VALQUEZ SEDUCTION
Melanie Milburne

PROTECTING THE DESERT PRINCESS
Carol Marinelli

ONE NIGHT WITH MORELLI
Kim Lawrence

TO DEFY A SHEIKH
Maisey Yates

THE RUSSIAN'S ACQUISITION
Dani Collins

THE TRUE KING OF DAHAAR
Tara Pammi

THE TWELVE DATES OF CHRISTMAS
Susan Meier

AT THE CHATEAU FOR CHRISTMAS
Rebecca Winters

A VERY SPECIAL HOLIDAY GIFT
Barbara Hannay

A NEW YEAR MARRIAGE PROPOSAL
Kate Hardy

MILLS & BOON®
Large Print – April 2015

TAKEN OVER BY THE BILLIONAIRE
Miranda Lee

CHRISTMAS IN DA CONTI'S BED
Sharon Kendrick

HIS FOR REVENGE
Caitlin Crews

A RULE WORTH BREAKING
Maggie Cox

WHAT THE GREEK WANTS MOST
Maya Blake

THE MAGNATE'S MANIFESTO
Jennifer Hayward

TO CLAIM HIS HEIR BY CHRISTMAS
Victoria Parker

SNOWBOUND SURPRISE FOR THE BILLIONAIRE
Michelle Douglas

CHRISTMAS WHERE THEY BELONG
Marion Lennox

MEET ME UNDER THE MISTLETOE
Cara Colter

A DIAMOND IN HER STOCKING
Kandy Shepherd

0315 Rom LP